The Last Bridesmaid

By PAMELA CARPENTER

Copyright © 2017 by Pamela Carpenter.
All rights reserved. No part of this publication may be reproduced, distributed, stored in a retrieval system, or transmitted in any form or by any means, including photocopying, recording, or electronic or mechanical methods, without the prior written permission of the publisher and copyright holder.

All characters in this book have no existence outside of the imagination of the author and have no relation whatsoever to anyone bearing the same name or names. They are not even distantly known or unknown to the author, and all incidents are pure invention. Any resemblance to actual events or locales or person, living or dead, is entirely coincidental.

Printed in the United States of America

To the loves of my life -

My husband and best friend, Luke.
Life got so much more fun when you came into it. I thank God every day for you.

Our beautiful son, Lukie.
Reach for the stars pumpkin. I did, and here you are - the greatest gift that I've ever received.

> When the world said "Give up"
> Hope whispered "Try it one more time."
>
> - Unknown

CHAPTER 1

It was a sunny Saturday afternoon in June on the Upper West Side of Manhattan, a perfect day for a wedding. A white Mercedes-Benz limo sat parked in front of the famous Riverside Church, with eight black Cadillac Escalades parked behind it that trailed down Riverside Drive.

Inside the church, cherry blossom tree branches decorated the numerous pillars that ran along the aisle. The church's massive organ, the fourteenth largest organ in the world, played Ave Maria with such power and beauty that the notes echoed throughout the church.

Seated in the pews were 250 stylishly dressed guests of the bride and groom, who had flown in from around the United States to help celebrate the happy couple. And standing up at the altar, were a nervous bride and a smitten groom, with bridesmaids and groomsmen to their left and right supporting them every step of the way.

Jules Alexander, the second bridesmaid on the left, began to pray during the musical selection.

> *God, I can't believe that I'm thirty-five years old, and I still haven't found my Mr. Right. And to make matters worse, this is my sixth time as a bridesmaid in the past five years. Talk about torture! God, when is it going to be my turn? When will I stop being the bridesmaid, and actually get to be the bride? It's not that I'm not happy for Maggie. I'm thrilled for her, actually. It's just getting harder and harder to keep standing up here watching my friends get their happy endings while I feel like I'm just withering away.*

Just then, the organ finished playing, and Jules snapped back to attention. Time to stop feeling sorry for herself and to go back to being happy for one of her best friends.

***

After the ceremony, the photographer had all of the bridesmaids lined up at the altar for pictures, while the bride, the groom, and the rest of the bridal party socialized in the pews with family members.

As the camera clicked away, Jules stood next to two other bridesmaids, Mylyn and Robin, who were also two of her best friends. They had all gone to Columbia University together with Maggie, the bride. Robin, who was six months pregnant, looked as though she was about to burst out of her bridesmaid's dress.

The three friends whispered out of the sides of their mouths, while posing for the photographer.

"Well ladies, it's down to you two!" whispered Robin to Mylyn and Jules.

"Oh no, not me. With today's divorce rate, are you kidding me? I don't even think I believe in marriage anymore," said Mylyn in a loud whisper.

"What about Andrew? You two have been dating for a while now," countered Robin.

"Please! Andrew can't even commit to what color socks to put on in the morning," joked Mylyn while posing for the next picture.

"Alright, big smiles everyone. On three. One, two, -" yelled out the photographer as he snapped the picture.

The camera flashed such a bright light that all of the bridesmaids squinted while trying to give their best smiles. After taking a second to recover from being temporarily blinded, the girls started whispering again.

"I think I blinked on that one," joked Mylyn.

"Anyway, men are more trouble than they're worth. Who needs 'em?" rationalized Jules.

"Hello! We do!" said Robin.

"Okay, last one. On three. One, two, -" interjected the photographer.

Everyone stopped and smiled for the cameras. And once again, the ladies squinted from the blinding flashes.

"Okay thanks everyone. That's a wrap for pictures here at the church. I'll take more shots of you at the reception," instructed the photographer as he looked over the shots that he'd just taken in his camera.

After being dismissed, Jules, Robin and Mylyn walked with the wedding party back outside and down the front steps of the church. The wedding guests were outside waiting to send off the bride and groom. They joyously blew bubbles as Maggie and Elton ran through the crowd and climbed into the waiting white limo. Everyone waved at the happy couple as the limo drove off down Riverside Drive. Then, the rest of the wedding party climbed into the eight chauffer driven Cadillac Escalades and pulled off after the limo.

***

About thirty minutes later, the limo and Escalades pulled up in front of the Plaza Hotel on Fifth Avenue in Midtown Manhattan. The bridal party and family members emerged from their cars and walked excitedly into the hotel for the wedding reception, still buzzing about what a beautiful wedding it had been.

***

Later, as the wedding reception was in full swing, Robin and Mylyn walked into the ladies room. They began touching up their make-up and hair in the mirror. There didn't seem to be anyone else in the bathroom with them.

"Hey, where's your hubby?" asked Mylyn.

"Arthur's working a big case so he had to work through the weekend. He hated having to miss Maggie's wedding," answered Robin.

"That sucks. So how much longer before little Arthur Jr. makes his way into the world?" asked Mylyn.

Robin patted her pregnant belly.

"Four more months to go. And there's still so much to do before the baby comes. Arthur and I have been going to doctor's appointments, and shopping for baby furniture, and painting the baby's room, and..." Robin was explaining before Mylyn cut her off.

"Sorry to cut you off hon', but does Jules seem okay to you?" asked Mylyn sounding concerned.

"Well, considering that this was her sixth time as a bridesmaid in the past five years - and she's still single - I'd say she's holding up pretty well," Robin responded.

"No, I'm talking about Lance the Lech. I can't believe that he had the nerve to show up here after what he did to Jules," said Mylyn.

"I know, right? And how could he bring that man-stealing witch with him?" Robin asked.

"Do you think Jules spotted them yet?" Mylyn asked.

Just then, Jules slowly emerged from one of the bathroom stalls. Mylyn and Robin were surprised since they didn't realize that Jules was in the bathroom and could hear them talking.

"He's here?" Jules asked stunned.

Mylyn and Robin looked at each other and then nodded in unison.

"And he brought... her?" Jules could barely get the words out.

Mylyn and Robin nodded again.

"Well where are they sitting?" asked Jules.

"Now Jules, don't go making a scene. It's in the past. Just let it stay there. Let's not ruin Maggie's big day," Robin begged.

"Where are they sitting?" Jules asked again getting irritated.

"Table 13," answered Mylyn.

"Well at least Maggie sat them in the back," said Jules.

Jules took a moment to think.

"Okay look, I'm not gonna hide in the bathroom all night. So I'm gonna go on out there and try to have some fun!" declared Jules as she walked out of the ladies room with her head held high.

Mylyn and Robin looked at each other with apprehension. They knew Jules, so they knew that something was about to go down. Robin and Mylyn exited from the ladies room and walked over to Jules, who was standing in the hallway right outside of the ballroom, where wedding guests were having a great time dancing on the dance floor.

A waiter stopped by the three bridesmaids with a tray of champagne.

"Champagne ladies?" the waiter offered cheerfully.

Jules and Mylyn both took a glass of champagne. Jules immediately began to drink the champagne as if she really needed a drink. Robin declined in her pregnant state. The waiter began to walk off, when Jules with a mouthful of champagne, motioned for the waiter to stay.

"Don't go anywhere. I'm just getting started," she said to the waiter as she gulped down her entire glass in seconds, and then grabbed another glass off of the waiter's tray.

"See, I'm having fun!" Jules said a little too convincingly.

She gulped down the second glass of champagne and grabbed a third.

"Don't you think you should slow down a little with the champagne?" Robin asked, concerned.

"Oh leave her alone. This is the first time that she's seen Lance in a year," Mylyn said, defending Jules.

"Who's Lance?" the waiter asked, joining in as if he was a part of the conversation.

"Lance is the lying, cheating, sonofobitch that Jules was engaged to," Mylyn explained.

"Yeah, until she caught him in bed with their wedding planner, Linda," Robin added.

"Damn! That's rough," the waiter said. "Here, have another glass of champagne on me," he said to Jules compassionately.

"And if that wasn't bad enough, Lance went and married that skank a few months after Jules kicked him to the curb," Mylyn explained to the waiter.

"Ouch! He sounds like a real piece of work!" the waiter said shaking his head.

"Excuse me! Can y'all stop talking about me like I'm not here? We're supposed to be having fun, remember? Now stop gossiping about me and let's go get our grooves on!" Jules said tipsy now. She was loosening up and starting to feel no pain.

"Well, good luck miss. I hope it all works out for you," said the waiter, and he walked back to the kitchen with a now empty tray.

Jules and her girlfriends walked through the reception in the huge ballroom, when Jules spotted Lance and Linda dancing on the dance floor.

"Well look who's here! There's Mr. Faithful and his blushing bride right over there," said a drunken Jules. "I think I'll go say hello," Jules handed her empty glass of champagne to a nervous Robin, who didn't really know what to do at that point. Then, while walking towards the dance floor, Jules picked up a glass of red wine from one of the tables, and walked over to Lance and Linda on the dance floor.

"Uh oh! What's she about to?" Robin said to Mylyn, who just stood there shaking her head.

Jules walked up to Lance and Linda, pretended to trip, and "accidentally" spilled the glass of red wine all over Linda's tight yellow dress. Linda screamed.

"Oh no! I'm so sorry," Jules said sarcastically. "I've been tripping over this dress all day."

Linda stood stunned and embarrassed on the dance floor with red wine dripping down the front of her dress.

"It was such a pretty dress too. Was that silk or a poly blend?" Jules asked with a big smile on her face. Linda fumed at the big red stain that was now in the center of her dress.

Lance stood smiling at Jules. He was thrilled to see her, and impressed by her spunk. He barely acknowledged that his wife was standing next to him drenched in red wine.

"Wow, Jules. You look amazing! How have you been?" asked Lance while looking Jules up and down. He'd forgotten how beautiful she was with her long, silky dark hair that fell to the middle of her back. And those lips. He'd missed kissing those luscious lips every day. He was still cursing himself for blowing it with her.

"Well Lance, I'm fantastic! Thanks for asking," Jules said sarcastically. She noticed him checking her out, and felt a bit of satisfaction that she could still turn his head.

But she still hated this man for blowing up their life together after a six year relationship. She looked at Lance like he was nothing. Like he'd never meant the world to her. Like she'd never wanted to marry him and have a family with him. Like she hadn't cried herself to sleep for months after he'd shattered her heart into a million pieces.

Jules walked off, and Lance couldn't take his eyes off of her. He just stood there staring at her longingly. He knew that he'd made a big mistake. But he'd made his bed and now he had to sleep in it.

An angry Linda had already started storming off towards the door to leave, but Lance was still frozen in place watching Jules.

"Lance, are you coming or what?!!?" Linda yelled at Lance in a demanding voice.

"Oh, yeah. Sure. I'll be right there," he said sounding a bit deflated. He walked towards the door, looked back one last time at Jules, and then left.

***

A few minutes later, Jules was dancing with a nerdy looking groomsman next to Mylyn, who was dancing with her boyfriend, Andrew.

"Girl, I still can't believe that you did that!" Mylyn said to Jules laughing.

"Hey look, she and her hooker-looking dress got off easy," laughed Jules.

Just then, the song ended and Jules and Mylyn walked off the dance floor to continue talking. The nerdy groomsman looked disappointed that he had just been abandoned without a second thought.

"Don't take it personally dude. You get used to it with these two," Andrew joked to the nerdy groomsman before he walked off towards the bar.

Jules and Mylyn went to sit down at the table where Robin was checking her emails on her cell phone.

"Did you see how Lance was looking at you?" Mylyn asked Jules.

"Oh? What are you talking about?" Jules asked, playing dumb.

"Girl, he couldn't take his eyes off of you. It looked like he still has feelings for you. Like maybe he realizes that he screwed up the best thing that ever happened to him," Mylyn continued.

"And he did not look happy to be leaving with Lap Dance Linda!" Robin joined in.

"Well, maybe he should've thought of that before he hopped in the sack with Miss Around-the-Way. He's the one who blew up our lives, so I hope he realizes what he missed out on," rationalized Jules.

"I still can't believe that Maggie let his stank ass come to the wedding," added Mylyn.

"Well he's still one of Elton's best friends, so I guess she had to invite him," said Jules.

"Actually, Maggie told me that Elton wanted to ask Lance to be one of his groomsmen, but Maggie knew that it would be too hard for you, so she told Elton 'hell no!'" confided Robin.

Just then, Maggie, the excited bride, hurried over to her bridesmaids.

"Okay Jules and Mylyn. I'm about to throw the bouquet, and I want my best single girlfriends front and center," squealed Maggie.

"Oh come on Magpie. You know how I hate that whole bouquet-throwing bit. It makes all single women look so desperate," complained Jules.

"Now Jules, stop being difficult and get your butt out there. This is Maggie's day, so whatever Maggie wants, Maggie gets," assisted Robin.

"Well Robin, that's easy for you to say since you're already married and don't have to submit yourself to this humiliation anymore," whined Jules.

"Come on Jules. Do it for me!" begged Maggie.

Maggie playfully grabbed Jules' hand and dragged her back out onto the dance floor, where there was a huddle of single women anxiously waiting for Maggie to throw the bouquet. Jules and Mylyn made their way towards the back of the huddle, not interested in making complete fools of themselves.

Maggie threw the bouquet over her shoulder towards the eager women, and a surprising brawl ensued. Once the bouquet was airborne, two overly aggressive women jumped up trying to grab it. They ended up tackling each other to the floor. The first woman grabbed the other woman by the hair and accidentally pulled out one of her hair extensions. The bouquet tumbled backwards, and another woman jumped up and grabbed it like it was a football at the Super Bowl.

Then, another woman grabbed the bouquet out of her hands, and the two women began yanking the bouquet back and forth in a frenzy. The bouquet fell backwards over their heads as other feisty women frantically tried to grab it.

Jules and Mylyn were standing towards the back during the commotion, when Jules accidentally got hit in the face by a stray elbow, which threw her backwards and landed her on the floor. After falling on her butt, the bouquet miraculously landed next to her, so Jules picked it up. She stood up with one hand holding the bouquet and the other hand over her eye.

"Oh my God Jules! Are you okay?" asked a concerned Mylyn. "What's the matter with these ghetto ass women?!!?"

***

Moments later, in the middle of the dance floor, Jules was seated on the lap of the nerdy groomsmen that she'd danced with earlier. As he had been the oh-so lucky single guy who'd caught Maggie's garter when Elton threw it minutes before, Jules was obligated to take a picture with him.

"Okay on three. Give me big smiles you two. One, two, -" yelled the photographer.

The camera flashed. Jules was holding the bride's bouquet while the nerdy groomsman was holding the garter. Jules looked pissed, wearing a fake smile and a black eye!

CHAPTER 2

It was Monday morning rush hour in Midtown Manhattan. Thousands of commuters speed-walked to work, while buses, yellow taxicabs and bike messengers sped down Park Avenue. Jules was dressed in a navy designer suit, gray sneakers, and black sunglasses as she walked quickly down the street with the other commuters. She carried a black canvas briefcase, and a black leather Michael Kors tote bag over her shoulder, along with her usual cup of Starbucks Chai Latte. Like the rest of New York City, Jules was in a hurry as she rushed into her 55-floor office building.

***

A few minutes later, Jules stepped off of the elevator onto the 52nd floor, and quickly walked through the double glass doors into the luxurious law offices of Dorfman & Whipley LLP. Still sporting her dark sunglasses, she was relieved to see that the receptionist was on the phone. She quickly walked down the hall to her office, hoping to not run into anyone.

A guy pushing a mail cart was walking down the hallway towards her. "Hey Jules. How was the wedding this weekend?" the mailroom guy asked.

"Oh it was so beautiful!" Jules responded cheerfully, and kept walking to avoid a long conversation.

As she walked down the hallway, an older woman walked towards Jules and stopped as if she was eager to chat. "Happy Monday darling! How was the wedding?" the woman inquired.

"Just peachy!" Jules said a little too short and kept walking. She had no intention of getting into a long chit chat session with the office gossip.

Jules eventually stopped at the desk of her assistant, Phyllis. "Good morning Phyllis. Any messages?" Jules asked trying to stay all business.

"Well, good morning yourself. Nope, no messages yet," Phyllis responded. "Hey, what's with the sunglasses? And how was the wedding on Saturday?"

"If one more person asks me how that damn wedding was, I'm going to scream!" Jules responded in a loud whisper. Phyllis' phone rang before she had a chance to inquire further. "Jules Alexander's office," Phyllis answered. Jules stomped off into her office, which was directly behind Phyllis' desk, and closed the door behind her.

Once inside, she walked across her spacious office to put her Chai Latte down on the mahogany desk that sat in front of a large window. There was an impressive view of Manhattan skyscrapers that illuminated her whole office. Then, she sat down on the couch that was along the wall, pulled a pair of heels out of her briefcase, kicked off her sneakers, and put the heels on.

She walked back over to her desk next and put her sneakers, briefcase and purse into her lower desk drawer, turned on her computer, and plopped down into her chair. She took a few sips of her Chai Latte, and spun around in her chair to gaze out the window.

Then, she took off her sunglasses, and pulled a compact out of her desk drawer. She looked into the compact's mirror and was disgusted that she still had a black eye left over from the wedding reception two nights before. She'd tried covering it up with make-up, but the bruise was so dark that it was still visible.

***

Later that morning, Jules was sitting at her desk typing on her computer when there was a knock at her door.

"Come in," Jules answered absentmindedly while still typing.

The door opened slightly and Charlie Rowland popped his head through. Charlie and Jules had started at the firm at the same time five years ago right out of law school. Jules was a few years older than Charlie though, since Jules had earned her MBA and worked on Wall Street before she went back to school to earn her JD.

Jules and Charlie had hit it off as co-workers when they first came into the firm. But, since Jules was in a relationship with Lance when they met, Charlie kept things platonic. Their friendship deepened, however, over the past year after Jules broke up with Lance. Charlie had become her rock and her shoulder to cry on whenever she felt overwhelmed. And unbeknownst to Jules, Charlie had been secretly in love with her since they met. Anyone who had ever witnessed them together could see it, but not Jules. She was completely oblivious to Charlie's romantic feelings for her.

"Hey gorgeous, how was the wedding?" he asked. "What the hell?" he said after catching a glimpse of Jules' shiner.

He came rushing into her office and closed the door behind him so no one else would see Jules' bruised eye. Jules looked at Charlie for a moment and dropped her head down on her desk in defeat.

"Damn Jules, what happened? Are you okay? Did you get into a fight? Did you get mugged?" he asked firing off questions at her.

"No, I caught the friggin' bouquet!" she answered sarcastically.

Charlie fell backwards onto Jules' couch and laughed hysterically. "I didn't know that you ladies could be so brutal about catching the bouquet. Maybe you should wear body armor to the next wedding that you go to" he said still laughing.

"Ha, ha, ha! Very funny Charlie Brown," she said with a smile starting to see the humor in the whole situation. "Anyway, something else happened."

"Oh no. I'm afraid to ask," he quipped.

"Lance was there... With Miss What's-Her-Name," she explained.

"You're kidding! So what happened? What did you do?" he asked intrigued, leaning forward on the couch as if he was planning to stay a while.

"I wish that I had time to give you all the juicy details, but I've got to finish preparing for a conference call. Can we talk about it over lunch?" she asked sounding rushed.

"Of course. We'll catch up later. Do you need some ice for that eye?" he asked concerned.

"You're so sweet, but no thanks. I iced this monstrosity all day yesterday," she responded as she waved him out of her office. "Now go. I've got a lot of work to do."

Charlie left, and Jules went back to typing on her computer.

***

At lunchtime, Charlie and Jules, with her black eye, were sitting at a table sharing a large chocolate milkshake with two straws. Charlie was laughing.

"I can't believe that you threw a glass of red wine at her! That's cold Jules!" he said still laughing.

"I didn't throw the wine at her. It was an accident, remember?" Jules said playfully.

"Yeah right. An accident. She's just lucky you didn't 'accidentally' run her over with your car!" Charlie said smiling. He and Jules were cracking up at Charlie's joke.

"How's your eye? Does it hurt?" Charlie asked.

"Not so much anymore. It was a lot worse yesterday," Jules answered.

Then, Charlie's mood shifted to a more serious tone.

"Okay, so now that you've gotten some closure on ol' boy, are you finally feeling ready to start dating again? It has been a year, you know," Charlie reasoned.

Just then, a waitress stopped by their table and left the check.

"I know. You're right. It's time for me to get back in the game, or else I'm gonna end up some dried up old maid," Jules said jokingly.

"Yeah right. Like that would ever happen. Have you seen how gorgeous you are?" Charlie said flirtatiously. But the flirtation was lost on Jules.

"But at least I don't have to worry about being the last of my friends to get married since Mylyn announced this past weekend that she's given up on marriage altogether," Jules declared.

Charlie handed the check and his credit card to the passing waitress.

"Anyway, that's enough about me. How was your weekend? Didn't you have a date lined up for Saturday night?" Jules asked.

"Uh, no that fell through," Charlie answered.

"You know, in the five years that we've been friends, I don't think that you've been a relationship that lasted longer than a few weeks," Jules observed.

Charlie's mood shifted. He seemed a little uncomfortable now.

"Well, maybe I've been taking a break from dating, just like you," Charlie said while picking up a half-eaten turkey sandwich and taking a bite.

"Are you sure that there isn't at least one special person that you think about?" she asked.

"Maybe there is someone, but she's been emotionally unavailable due to her own situation," he said as he took another bite of his sandwich and then joked, "Maybe I'm just waiting for that special girl to be ready for my affections."

"Oh Charlie, stop playing with me. Is there someone or not?" Jules cluelessly asked.

Charlie stood up from the booth as if he was ready to leave. He held his hand out to Jules.

"If there is someone, believe me, you'll be the first to know. Now come on. We've gotta get back to work. I'm due in court in an hour."

Jules took Charlie's hand as she stood, and they walked out of the diner.

Later that night, a black Lincoln Towncar pulled up to Jules' high rise apartment building on the Upper West Side. She emerged from the back seat, still dressed in her work clothes. The Towncar pulled off and Jules walked into her building, exhausted from a long day of work.

***

A few minutes later, Jules entered her apartment and turned on the lights. She walked into her living room, and put her briefcase and purse down on the floor next to a beige faux suede couch as she sat down and kicked off her sneakers. Her apartment was very modern and stylish, yet comfortable at the same time. In the living room, there was a huge window that provided a stunning view of the Hudson River with the George Washington Bridge lit up in the distance.

Jules walked into the kitchen, got a pint of Butter Pecan ice cream out of the freezer and grabbed a spoon from a drawer. Then, she walked in her stocking feet back into the living room and plopped down on her couch. She put the ice cream and spoon down on the coffee table in front of her, and reached into her purse for her cell phone. She dialed into her voicemail, pushed the speakerphone button, and put the phone down on the coffee table. She picked the pint of ice cream back up and started to enjoy her nighttime ritual, while waiting for the first voicemail message to play.

> *Hi honey, it's Mom. I just wanted to give you a call to see how Maggie's wedding was on Saturday. I'm sure you looked*

beautiful in your bridesmaid's dress.

Jules listened to her Mom's voicemail while eating her ice cream.

By the way, when are you going to trade up to a wedding gown? Your father and I don't want to be too old to play with our grandkids you know!

At that, Jules shoveled an extra-large spoonful of ice cream into her mouth. "Oh come on Mom, give it a rest already!" Jules mumbled to herself with a mouth full of Butter Pecan.

Anyway, give me a call back when you get a chance. I want to hear all the details, okay? Love you. Bye,

Jules picked up the phone and hit the delete button.

Then, she walked back to the kitchen, put the ice cream back in the freezer, and walked past her living room into her bedroom with her phone.

She hit a button to hear the next voicemail and she walked to her dresser, where she pulled out a Columbia University tee shirt and sweatpants as the next message played.

> *Good afternoon Miss Alexander, I'm calling from Dr. Marshall's office to remind you that it's time for your annual check-up. Please give our office a call at (212)555-2334 to schedule an appointment. We look forward to hearing from you soon.*

Jules picked up her phone and hit delete. Then, she took off her suit jacket to start changing out of her work clothes, when the next message began to play.

> *Oh my God Jules! It's Mylyn. Call me back as soon as you get this message. I have to tell you something... and it's huge!*

Mylyn's voice sounded frantic.

Jules stopped undressing as the next message played.

Dammit Jules, where are you? I have to tell you something big or I'm gonna burst! Call me back ASAP!

Mylyn practically yelled giddily in her message.

Jules unbuttoned her blouse and yelled out loud to herself "Damn, just tell me already!"

The next message began to play as Jules stepped out of her skirt.

Okay, obviously your cell phone is turned off and I can't wait for you to get out of court to turn the damn thing back on. So, I'm just gonna have to tell you my news on your stupid voicemail,

Mylyn paused for effect.

Andrew asked me to marry him tonight! Can you believe it?

Jules, now down to her black lacy underwear, absentmindedly fell onto her bed in shock. She couldn't believe what she was hearing.

> *Jules, he was so sweet and romantic, and he even got down on one knee and everything! And girl, you should see the ring... Daaaaamn!!! It's sooooo sparkly and beautiful! I can't stop looking at it on my finger!*

Jules still sitting in her underwear was staring at her phone with her mouth half open in disbelief at what she was hearing.

> *Oh yeah, and of course I said 'Yes!' And you're not gonna believe this next part, but we've already set a date! We've decided to get married on the anniversary of the day that we met, which just happens to be in sixty days!*

"What?!!!?" Jules yelled at her phone.

> *I know that it's just a couple of months away, so obviously we're gonna keep the ceremony small. I already talked to my mom and we're gonna have it at my parents' house in Westchester. I was thinking that their garden would be a perfect setting. I've always wanted a garden wedding.*

Jules sat incredulously on her bed still listening to this crazy message.

> *Anyway, I would love it if you would be one of my bridesmaids. Give me a call tomorrow so we can talk more since you're obviously working late again. Jules, I can't believe I'm getting married! Whoo hoo! Okay, call me tomorrow. Bye!*

Jules turned off the speaker phone and started pacing as a panic started to build. Then, she started talking to herself.

"Mylyn is getting married? But she just said this weekend that she didn't believe in marriage anymore. And, she said that Andrew wouldn't commit. So what happened?"

Jules continued to pace. She was working herself up into a frenzy. She walked over to the mirror on her living room wall and shook her head as she examined her fading black eye. Then, she started talking to herself in the mirror.

"You know what this means right? You're gonna be the last single girl in your crew... In New York City!... In the whole friggin' world!!! I'm going to be an old maid. I'll probably have a bunch of cats to keep me company and all the kids on the block will call me that old cat lady who lives in 22C!" Jules said feeling sorry for herself.

Then, while deep in a daydream, Jules' reflection in the mirror seemed to come to life. She was a calmer, more confident version of Jules in her current state of mind.

"No you won't," Jules' reflection said. "You're allergic to cats, remember?"

Jules jumped at the sound of her own voice talking back to her.

"Who was that?" Jules whispered to no one in particular.

She started looking around her apartment trying to figure out where the voice came from. She looked under her couch. Then she looked under the pillows on her couch as if the voice could be coming from there.

"You know who I am, right?" Jules' reflection asked from the mirror.

"God?" Jules answered completely clueless. She looked up at the ceiling as if expecting God to appear.

"No dummy. Over here," Jules refection responded.

Jules looked over at the mirror and was in shock to see her own reflection looking back at her, but as a separate person. She walked cautiously over to the mirror.

"Who are you?" Jules asked slowly.

"I'm you silly," her refection answered.

"Ok, now I know that I'm losing it! It's already starting. I'm gonna grow old alone with no one to talk to except my crazy lonely self," Jules said as if thinking out loud.

"Well what am I? Chopped liver?" Jules' reflection asked trying to cheer Jules up. Jules still didn't fully accept that her reflection was talking back to her.

"Oh dear Lord! I'm one step away from the looney bin!" Jules said to herself.

She walked away from the mirror and went into the kitchen. She opened the freezer, took a different pint of ice cream out, and grabbed a spoon out of the dishwasher.

A few seconds later, Jules walked back out to the living room eating out of a pint of Baskin & Robbins with another big spoon. She walked back to the couch in the living room and plopped down, still eating her ice cream. Jules starts talking to herself with a mouthful of Pralines & Cream.

"How did this happen to me?" Jules pondered. "Last year, I was about to be married to someone that I thought was the man of my dreams, and this year, I'm an old maid."

"Psst. Will you put that ice cream down and get a hold of yourself? This isn't the time for you to be ruining our figure. We've got work to do," Jules' reflection said from the mirror.

"What do you mean 'we've' got work to do?" Jules asked.

"Well, the way that I see it, if you don't want to be the last one married, then don't be. All you have to do is find a husband before Mylyn says 'I do'," Jules' reflection offered.

"Are you nuts? Did you miss the part when Mylyn said that she's getting married in sixty days?" Jules practically yelled at the mirror feeling a bit unhinged.

"Yes, I heard her. So what's your point?" the reflection asked.

"What's my point? How am I supposed to meet the man of my dreams, fall in love, and get married in two months? It's impossible!" Jules yelled at the mirror.

"Difficult maybe, but not impossible. Nothing is impossible. You just need a good strategy. Come on Jules. You're a smart girl. Treat this like any other goal that you've ever set for yourself. Map out a plan, stay focused, and don't give up until you get what you want," the reflection said giving Jules a pep talk.

Jules thought to herself for a moment, then seemed to find a renewed energy.

"You know what? You're right. That business with Lance was over a year ago, and I've been hiding out ever since. It's time for me to stop feeling sorry for myself and get back out there. So what if I've only got two months to find a husband. I've faced bigger challenges than that, right?" Jules reasoned sounding inspired.

"Trust me. With our looks and brains, we'll be Mrs. Somebody by the end of the week!" the reflection joked.

"Yeah!" Jules agreed, and stuffed her face with more ice cream.

CHAPTER 3

The next morning, Jules stepped off of the elevator at work and walked down the hallway towards her office. She carried her purse, briefcase and Starbucks Chai Latte as she did every morning. But this morning in particular, she walked cheerfully down the hallway. She was in a good mood. Her black eye had disappeared while she was sleeping, and she was a woman on a mission to find her Mr. Right over the next couple of months. Life was about to get really exciting.

She saw Charlie, who spotted her from the other end of the hallway and walked towards her.

"Hey love, who lit your feet on fire this morning?" he asked playfully.

"Oh good, Charlie. I'm glad that I ran into you. I need your help," Jules said.

"Sure. You know that I'm here for whatever you need. What's up?" Charlie responded.

"Well, I'm working on a new project that I could use your help with.

But no one, and I mean absolutely no one, can know about it," she said.

Charlie was suspicious that Jules was up to another one of her crazy ideas. Since he'd known her, she typically came up with a new wacky scheme every six months or so.

"Uh huh," he replied carefully.

"Walk with me," Jules said.

Jules and Charlie walked down the hall and went into Jules' office. Jules closed the door behind them. She walked behind her desk and turned on the computer. Jules stashed her purse and briefcase in her desk drawer, put her Starbucks cup on the desk, opened the blinds to let in the morning sun, and sat down behind her desk.

Charlie plopped down on the couch anxious to hear what Jules had up her sleeve.

"So, what's this mystery project that you're working on?" he asked.

"The project is that I have two months to find the man that I'm going to marry. And I need your help to find him," Jules revealed.

"Cute. No seriously, what's the project?" Charlie responded. He thought that she was joking, because there was no way that she could be serious.

"I'm serious. You know my girl Mylyn?" she asked.

"Mm hmm," Charlie responded not sure where Jules was going with this.

"Well, she called me last night to tell me that she's getting married and she wants me to be a bridesmaid in her wedding. Can you believe that?" Jules said starting to get worked up again.

"Well, you two have been friends since college," Charlie said still not sure where Jules' head was.

"This will be my seventh time as a bridesmaid in the past five years! Seventh!!!" she said exasperated.

Charlie still didn't get why Jules was so upset. He still wasn't taking her seriously.

"Okay," he said slowly like he was talking to someone who'd lost her marbles. "I still don't understand why Mylyn getting married has gotten you all riled up. I thought that women got off on being asked to be bridesmaids. So what's the problem?" he asked.

"Yeah, maybe the first or second time, but seven times? I'm tired of standing on the sidelines cheering the happy couple on, while I'm secretly dying inside because I haven't found someone to share my life with," she explained. "I need to get back in the game."

"So let me see if I understand this. You swore off dating for a whole year after Lance Jerkweed, and now you want to go to the other extreme and find a husband in two months?" Charlie asked. "Is it me, or have you completely lost your mind?"

"Look, Mylyn is getting married fifty-nine days from now. And I'll be damned if I'm gonna be the last single woman at her wedding!" Jules declared.

"First of all, you won't be the last single woman at her wedding. And second of all, do you know how crazy you sound?" Charlie asked.

"Not crazy. Determined! I was up all night thinking about it, and I think that the reason that I haven't found 'the one' yet is because I haven't been looking," Jules announced.

"Well, duh!" Charlie replied sarcastically. He was starting to feel offended that Jules wasn't considering that maybe he might be the man for her after he's been on the sidelines for a year waiting for her to heal from her broken engagement.

"I'm always working late or hanging out with you or my girlfriends. After that whole Lance disaster, I should've just gotten right back on the horse and started dating again, not hiding out the way that I have been. And now, I'm in danger of heading into old maid-hood," she reasoned.

"So what are you planning?" Charlie asked, almost afraid to hear her answer.

"Well, online dating seems to be where it's at now. I'm thinking that'll be the best place to start looking," she answered.

"Jules, you've really lost it," Charlie sighed.

Lost in her thoughts, Jules ignored Charlie's skepticism. She began typing on her computer.

"I started looking at some online dating websites last night, and I narrowed it down to these," she said.

Charlie walked around Jules' desk to read her computer screen.

MateFinders.com
Lovebirds.com
IHateBeingSingle.com

"Come on Jules, this is cheezy!" Charlie replied.

"No it isn't. My girl Christine found her husband on one of these sites. Now stop being so negative and help me put a profile together," Jules cutely ordered.

Charlie sat on the window sill behind Jules' desk.

"No, I'm not going to help you with this hair-brained scheme! Don't you know that you'll meet all kinds of ax-murderers this way? These websites bring out the crazies. Is that what you want?" Charlie asked, trying to talk some sense into his friend.

"Charlie pleeeeaasse!" Jules sweetly said trying to soften Charlie up.

"Jules, have you looked in the mirror lately? You're gorgeous! And you're smart, and funny, and sexy. You don't need to go at it this way. You could have any guy you want. In fact, there's probably some poor shlub who's already head-over-heels for you who's been right in front of you the whole time. Maybe if you stopped looking everywhere else, you might actually notice him," Charlie hinted.

Jules thought for a second, and then started typing on her computer again.

"Yeah right. Thanks for the pep talk, but obviously that isn't true since I'm still single," Jules said oblivious to the passive aggressive confession that Charlie had just made.

"Look, we're losing precious time talking this to death. I've got to fill out this profile before my ten o'clock meeting," Jules said while typing. She stopped and began to read the computer screen.

"Okay, here's the first question, 'What type of relationship are you seeking?' Choose Long-Term, Casual, or Any'. I'm choosing 'Long-Term'," Jules said as she typed in her response.

"This is stupid. I'm going back to my office. Some of us actually have real work to do this morning," Charlie said feeling a bit rejected.

Jules was barely listening to Charlie since she was so engrossed in creating her profile on the website.

"Yeah ok. I'll catch up with you later," she said distracted. "Next question, 'Sexual Orientation - Heterosexual? Homosexual? Bisexual?"

Jules continued to type away on her computer as Charlie walked out of Jules' office shaking his head in disbelief.

***

Later that evening, still at work, Jules walked down the hall to Charlie's office. Charlie was reading some papers in a file. Jules stopped in his doorway and he looked up.

"I haven't seen you leave work this early in months," Charlie said.

"Well it is seven o'clock. Most non-lawyers are probably already at home eating dinner with their families," she quipped.

"So are you on your way home?" he asked.

"Nope. I have a date," she answered.

"A date? With who?" Charlie asked surprised.

"Well, actually I've lined up a few dates for tonight," she announced, proud of herself.

"I'm sorry, what?" Charlie responded.

"I finished my profile and posted it on MateFinders.com this morning, and by this afternoon I had fourteen responses! Can you believe it?" Jules said excitedly.

"Really," Charlie deadpanned.

"Yep. So, I'm going to meet my first few dates tonight down at Luke's," she explained further ignoring Charlie's less than enthusiastic attitude.

"I can't believe that you're really going through with this. What do you think is going to happen Jules? Do you really think that you're gonna meet some guy and get to know him well enough to know that you want to spend the rest of your life with him in sixty days?" he asked trying not to lose his temper.

"Remember, I'm down to fifty-nine days," Jules responded playfully.

"And even if you had psychic powers, and it was love at first site, do you really think that any decent guy would marry someone that he just met?" Charlie was really trying to get through to her.

"Charlie, it's possible," Jules responded a little defensively.

"Please! He would think you were insane, which is what I'm starting to think that you are, and he'd run for the hills!" Charlie said trying to give her a dose of reality.

"Will you stop thinking so negatively? You never know unless you try, right?" she reasoned.

Charlie just stared at her in disbelief.

"Anyway, good chat. Wish me luck. I've gotta run so that I'm not late for my first date," Jules said proudly and she rushed off down the hall towards the elevators.

"Yeah, good luck," Charlie said to himself.

***

Luke's Bar & Grill was part restaurant part karaoke bar that was only a couple of blocks away from Jules' office. She and Charlie often went there with co-workers for Happy Hour after work. It was a bit of a hole-in-the-wall, but the drinks and appetizers were good, and who could resist a night of bad singing after a long day of work?

Jules was sitting in a booth talking to a pale, extremely skinny, strange looking man with slightly spiked hair named Norman. They each had drinks in front of them. Jules looked really bored, while Norman looked eager to impress Jules.

"You'd be surprised at how often opportunities for a professional whistler come up," Norman said. "I've whistled for TV and radio commercials, movies, and I've even been hired to whistle at a few weddings," he declared proudly.

"Really. That sounds fascinating," Jules responded. She was trying to be polite, but actually she thought that this guy was a little creepy.

"If you want, I can belt you out a tune. Do you know 'Ribbons in the Sky' by Stevie Wonder?" he eagerly asked.

Before Jules could answer, Norman began to whistle "Ribbons in the Sky". Jules looked embarrassed that this weirdo was whistling a love song to her in a public place. There was a couple at the next table that stopped eating a platter of chicken wings when they heard the whistling. They looked at Jules with sympathy that she had such a dud for a date.

Jules stopped Norman in the middle of his whistling serenade.

"Oh Norman, that was beautiful. But listen, I've got to get up early in the morning. So, I'm going to have to call it a night," Jules lied.

Poor Norman looked disappointed.

"Oh, okay. I had a nice time. What are you doing tomorrow night?" Norman asked hopefully.

"Um, I think that I'm going to be working late. But I'll call you if my schedule frees up," Jules lied, as she stood up and walked to the bathroom to hide out until Norman left.

***

Thirty minutes later, Jules was sitting at the same booth at Luke's with her second date of the evening, Clyde, who looked to be about seventy years old. He was dressed in a white suit with a blue collared shirt that was buttoned way too low, and revealed a chest full of gray hairs and a gold chain. Jules mused that he must've been a big *Miami Vice* fan from back in the 80s. Again, she looked as though she couldn't wait for the date to be over.

Up on the stage behind them, a tipsy woman dressed in a suit with slightly disheveled hair was belting out a butchered version of the Gloria Gaynor classic, "I Will Survive." Her co-workers, who all looked like a bunch of burned out lawyers, were drunk and cheering her on. The more terrible her singing was, the louder they cheered. They were having fun blowing off some steam from their long day.

"I know that I'm a little older than my profile picture, but I like my ladies young," said Clyde as he winked at Jules.

"Is that so?" Jules said trying to keep from laughing. As amusing as Clyde was, she was also annoyed that she'd been duped. The picture that Clyde had posted was of a man who was about thirty years younger. "By the way, who was that man in the profile picture that you posted?"

"Oh, that was me back in 1988. I've always loved that picture. I was in my prime back in those days," Clyde said with pride.

Just then a waitress walked over with a large tray of food.

"Okay, for the lady we've got one Caesar salad with grilled chicken," said the waitress as she placed the salad in front of Jules.

"And for your father, we've got a double bacon barbecue cheeseburger with everything on it, a loaded baked potato, the full rack of baby-back ribs, a side of chili cheese fries, and a large chocolate shake," finished the waitress as she struggled to find enough space on the table to put all of Clyde's food.

"Mmmm. Looks good!" said Clyde with excitement. He was so happy to see the food, that he missed the waitress' error of calling Clyde Jules' father.

"Can I get you anything else?" asked the waitress politely.

"I don't think there's any more room on the table!" Jules joked trying to have fun on another date from hell.

The waitress walked off as Clyde tore into the burger like he hadn't eaten in a year.

"Wow, Clyde. You sure do have a big appetite," Jules observed.

"Oh yeah, it's the Viagra. It always gives me the munchies." Clyde winked at Jules again and woofed down a handful of chili cheese fries.

***

Later that night, Jules was still at Luke's Bar & Grill sipping on a Midori Sour, sitting in the same booth as her two failed dates. This time, there was a middle aged man up on the stage singing his heart out to Frank Sinatra's "I Did It My Way." He was there with a birthday party, and his friends were cracking up at his bad singing.

Then, Jules' next date walked up to her wearing some kind of black leather outfit that consisted of a black leather jacket and black leather pants, with a black leather hat to match. And to top it all off, he wore a pair of mirrored aviator sunglasses to really nail down his look. Jules wasn't sure if he was trying out to be in a motorcycle gang, or to be the next lead singer of the Village People.

"Oh hell no!" is all that she managed to say before she stood up and walked away, leaving her black leather Romeo standing alone at the booth.

***

Minutes later, Jules was sitting alone at the bar at Luke's. She had an empty glass in front of her with an umbrella sticking out of it. She was tipsy, and was leaning on one elbow. She was telling her sorrows to Rob, the bartender. Since she was a Luke's regular, she and Rob had gotten to know each other a bit over the years.

"Rob, at this rate, I'm never gonna find him," Jules said, slightly slurring her words.

"Who?" asked Rob, who was a little amused at Jules' drunken behavior.

"Him! The One. My knight in shining armor. My Mr. Right! You know," Jules explained as if she was making perfect sense.

"Ohhh. Is that why you were here hanging out with all of those jokers tonight?" Rob asked.

"Yep. Turns out everyone lies in their online profile," Jules responded half-joking at her naiveté.

"Jules, you know that the whole soul mate thing is a myth, right?" Rob advised.

"Well Rob, if it's such a myth, then how come all of my friends are either married or engaged?" Jules responded feeling sorry for herself.

"They might be married, but are they happy? There's a difference," Rob retorted trying to cheer Jules up.

"Yeah, yeah, yeah. The difference is that they have someone to share their lives with, and I'm all alone," Jules said sadly. "Hit me again will ya?"

Jules picked up her empty glass and pointed it at Rob.

"Uh uh. No more Midori Sours for you doll. I'm cutting you off," Rob said thoughtfully.

"Oh come on Robbie! My night was a complete disaster. I came in here thinking that I was gonna meet three princes and all I ended up with were three frogs," Jules said starting to laugh as she thought about the humor of it all.

Just then, Charlie walked into Luke's Bar, and he made a beeline for Jules as soon as he spotted her. Jules was surprised to see him.

"Hey, where'd you come from?" Jules asked Charlie, still slurring her words.

"Thanks Rob for calling me," Charlie said to Rob as they slapped hands over the bar.

"No problem man. Just get her home safe and sound," Rob said.

"Hey, I don't need a babysitter!" Jules said.

"Okay, come on Sunshine! I've got an Uber out front," Charlie said as he gently took Jules' hand and led her out of Luke's Bar & Grill.

***

A few minutes later, Charlie and Jules walked up the hallway to Jules' front door. Charlie was holding Jules up as she giggled in her tipsy state. He had her key in his hand, but he was struggling to get her key into the lock to open the door. As if he weren't having a hard enough time getting the door unlocked, Jules began to tickle him trying to be playful.

"Will you stop it?" Charlie said trying not to laugh.

"Oh come on Charlie Brown. You know you're ticklish," Jules said laughing.

Charlie was still trying not to laugh, but he started to laugh a little bit.

"I am not. Now stop it before I drop you!" Charlie said like a father scolding a misbehaving child.

"Oh you're no fun Mr. Charlie and the Chocolate Factory!" Jules teased.

Charlie finally got the door open and he carried a drunk Jules inside to the living room. She was laughing hysterically trying to tickle him again as Charlie flicked on the light switch. He carried her over to the couch and put her down thoughtfully. He then walked into the kitchen, leaving Jules in the living room alone.

"You're no fun! You never wanna play! Always Mr. Serious. Mr.

Responsible. Why don't you just live a little?" Jules yelled to Charlie, who was in the kitchen fidgeting around.

Jules stood up and staggered over to the mirror and started staring at it from different angles. She was looking for her alter ego, who had spoken to her the night before. But the mirror had gone back to normal. No more talking reflection.

Jules started to walk away from the mirror, and then spun around quickly as if she was trying to catch her alter ego by surprise. But the mirror was still just a mirror. No talking reflection. After a few seconds, Jules gave up and walked back to the couch, where she plopped down onto it.

Just then, Charlie walked out of the kitchen holding a glass of water. He put the glass down onto the coffee table in front of Jules.

"Oh is that what you were doing? Setting up dates with desperate losers is what you call living it up?" Charlie stuck back at Jules' dig.

"Ooh, I think Charlie Chaplin may be a little bit jealous," Jules teased.

"What are you talking about?" Charlie responded, brushing off Jules' drunken analysis.

Then, he walked into Jules' bedroom to get to the bathroom. He opened up her medicine cabinet and took out a bottle of Tylenol.

Back in the living room, Jules was yawning.

"Well, you've been giving me a hard time all day about my husband search," Jules yelled towards her bedroom. She stretched out her arms and gave a big yawn.

"Right! Like I should be jealous of some old player who watched *Saturday Night Fever* one too many times," Charlie yelled back from the bathroom. "Yeah, Rob told me all about your so-called 'dates' when he called me. You sure know how to pick 'em," he laughed.

Jules didn't respond. When Charlie walked back into the living room with a Tylenol bottle, he discovered that Jules had fallen asleep on the couch. He sat down next to her and gently took off her heels. Then, he took a beige throw blanket off of the back of the couch and draped it over her. Charlie smiled to himself as he gazed at his beautiful friend.

"What am I going to do with you?" Charlie whispered to a sleeping Jules.

He sat for a moment watching her sleep, before leaning over and kissing her lightly on the forehead. Then he stood up, walked over and switched the lights off. He looked back at the sleeping beauty one last time before he left Jules' apartment, closing the door slowly behind him.

***

The next afternoon, Jules was in her office popping a couple of alka seltzers into a glass of water. Looking exhausted and hung over, she took a long drink from the glass and moaned. Then, she slowly walked over to the couch as if every step was causing her head to hurt more and she slowly laid down. She took one of the throw pillows off of the couch and put it over her face. Just then, there was a knock at the door.

"Go away!" Jules gave a muffled moan from under the pillow.

Her assistant, Phyllis, walked in and looked sympathetic.

"You poor thing. You look like death today," Phyllis offered.

"Gee, thanks," Jules responded with her face still under the pillow.

"Do you need some aspirin or something?" Phyllis asked trying to be helpful to her boss.

"No thanks. I've already taken some Tylenol," Jules said gratefully.

"So, how did it go in court this morning?" Phyllis asked genuinely curious as to how Jules was able to perform well in court with such a bad hangover.

Jules took the pillow off of her face slowly as her eyes tried to adjust to the light in her office.

"We won! The judge ruled in our favor thank goodness," Jules announced. "Lucky for me, I suffer from delayed hangovers. So, my headache didn't hit me until after I left court and I got back to the office. Now I feel like I got hit by a truck!" she said. "What was I thinking drinking those five Midori Sours? I'm not even a big drinker," Jules went on.

"So Mr. Braithwaite was happy I take it?" Phyllis asked encouragingly.

"That's an understatement. The judge awarded Mr. Braithwaite back-pay and punitive damages of $250,000 for wrongful termination. So he's thrilled!" Jules declared.

"That's great news! Congratulations!" said Phyllis.

"Well thank you. I'm glad to be checking another case off in the win column," said Jules proudly.

With this, Phyllis left Jules' office and walked back out to her desk. Jules put the pillow back over her face. After a few seconds, there was another knock at the door. Jules mumbled to herself in frustration that she couldn't seem to squeeze in a few moments to herself.

"What is this, Grand Central Station?" Jules said sarcastically to herself from under the pillow. "Come in," she yelled in a muffled voice.

Charlie walked in and closed the door. He stood over Jules for a second, shaking his head while Jules lay on the couch with a pillow over her face.

"Hey you!" he said cheerfully.

Jules didn't move. Her face was still under the pillow.

"Hey yourself!" she said in a muffled voice.

"I stopped by earlier to check on you, but you were in court all morning. Congrats by the way. I heard about your sweet victory," Charlie offered.

"Thank you! That's why they pay me the big bucks!" Jules said jokingly.

"Jules, take that pillow off of your face so I can talk to you for a minute," Charlie said in a serious tone.

Jules lowered the pillow. She looked worn out.

"Damn! You look like you got hit by a train!" Charlie said laughing.

"Yep, that's exactly how I feel," Jules agreed.

"What are you taking for that nasty hangover?" Charlie asked playfully concerned.

"I just took a couple of alka seltzers a few minutes ago. I'm just waiting for them to kick in," Jules responded in what was almost a whisper.

Charlie looked a little nervous as if there was something important that he wanted to confess.

"Maybe this isn't the best time to talk to you then," Charlie said, starting to lose his nerve.

"I feel like crap, but you know that you can always talk to me. What's up?" Jules asked thoughtfully.

Charlie started to pace a little as if he was trying to get his courage up to spit out whatever it was that he wanted to say.

"Okay, well... We've been friends for a few years now, right?" Charlie asked nervously.

"Uh huh," Jules responded.

"And we've gotten pretty close, right?" Charlie asked, still beating around the bush.

"Like two peas in a pod," Jules said smiling at Charlie to give him encouragement to spill whatever he was trying to say.

"Yeah. Peas in a pod. But listen, all of this running around town looking for a man... Well, it's just so unnecessary," Charlie said trying to get to his point.

"Oh yeah? Why's that?" Jules asked.

"Because there are people that already care about you that you're overlooking," Charlie hinted.

"People?" Jules asked suspiciously and still clueless.

"Yeah. People," Charlie responded almost tripping over his own feet while pacing in front of Jules.

"People, like who?" Jules asked.

"Like who?" he asked rhetorically.

Charlie was blowing it with his nervousness. He was in love with Jules, but Jules was oblivious to his feelings. She had him securely tucked away in the dreaded "friends zone", and now she didn't see him as anything more than just a good friend. And because he was afraid that she wouldn't return his feelings if he revealed them, he was having a hard time telling her how he truly felt. He was afraid of losing her.

"Well, there are men that you may have only thought of as friends, who maybe decided not to make a move on you because you were nursing a broken heart over that joker, Lance," Charlie said, starting to make some progress.

"Okay," Jules said slowly, trying to figure out where Charlie was heading with this.

"And, maybe if you gave them a chance, you might find the special relationship that you're looking for," Charlie continued. "So that's why I wanted to tell you -"

Just then, Jules' cell phone rang. She looked at the caller ID on her phone's screen.

"I'm sorry, hold that thought. I've been waiting for this call," Jules said as she picked up her cell phone.

"Jules Alexander," she answered. "Yes hi!... Robin told me that she gave you my number... Well, I'm looking forward to meeting you too... 7:30 next Thursday night sounds great!... Yes, I know exactly where that is... Okay, I'll meet you there... Me too... Okay, bye."

Jules hung up and walked over to her desk to write something down on a Post-It. Charlie, who had been sitting on the couch listening to Jules' phone conversation looked upset.

"You're going out on another date tonight?" he fumed.

"Well no. Actually, tonight I'm going to a speed dating party," she answered.

Charlie looked frustrated.

"That call was from Robin's cousin, Chase. She set me up on a blind date with him for next week," she explained. "He's taking me to the theatre," Jules said with a mock British accent.

"How are you going out tonight with that nasty hangover?" Charlie asked, looking for excuses to keep her from going out.

"The alka seltzers are kicking in now, so I should be okay," Jules answered walking around to the other side of her desk and sitting down to type on her computer.

"I don't believe you!" Charlie said, frustrated. He stood up from the couch and stormed towards the door.

"Hey, where are you going? Why are you getting mad? I thought you wanted to talk?" Jules called out to him.

"Never mind. Obviously this is a bad time," Charlie sulked as he walked out of her office.

Jules looked confused for a second before shrugging it off. She walked back over to her couch, laid back down, and covered her face again with a pillow.

CHAPTER 4

Later that evening, the speed dating party was being held in a round-shaped rotunda with high ceilings. There were forty people seated at tables that were arranged in one big circle. There were twenty men seated on the outside of the circle and twenty women seated on the inside. A male moderator walked around the room with a medium sized gong bell that he rang every five minutes to signal the speed daters when it was time to shift over for their next date.

Jules was talking to a guy named Joe, who was sitting across from her at the round table. He was a really tall man, with a stature of about six foot five inches. They seemed to be having an awkward conversation.

"Yes, I'm an attorney specializing in Labor Law. And what do you do Joe?" Jules asked politely, already knowing that she felt absolutely no attraction to this man.

"I'm a writer," Joe answered in a deep bellowing voice.

"Oh wow! How exciting. Do you write books, or plays or movies?" Jules asked enthusiastically, hoping to have found something interesting to talk about.

"No, I write greeting cards," Joe answered.

Jules was surprised by Joe's response since she'd never met anyone who wrote greeting cards before. In fact, she'd never even thought about who wrote the greeting cards that she'd been buying for years. She paused for a moment to try to think of something nice to say.

"You know, I don't think that I've ever met anyone who does what you do," Jules finally said after a few seconds of awkward silence.

"Yeah well, it pays the bills," Joe said sounding almost depressed. His personality was a real buzz kill.

"Do you have a specialty? I mean, do you specialize in funny cards, or romantic ones? Birthday cards or anniversary cards? I would think that there'd be so many genres to write for,"

Jules said, trying to keep the conversation going.

"I write all of that romantic crap that you see on the shelves for anniversaries and weddings, plus the holiday that I hate the most, Valentine's Day," he responded. It was clear that he hated his job and he hated romance even more. So what was he doing at a speed dating event?

"So Joe, have you ever been married?" she asked anxious to change the subject.

"Once. But it didn't work out," Joe said depressingly.

"Oh, I'm sorry. If you don't mind my asking, what went wrong?" Jules didn't want to pry, but in speed dating, the participants only got five minutes to ask questions before the moderator rang the bell, and then they had to move on to the next person.

"Well, she was always harping on me to take out the garbage, or to walk the dog, or to pick something up from the store on the way home from work. Just nag, nag, nagging me all the time!" he answered sounding a bit angry as if he were reliving his nightmarish marriage all over again.

"I'm sorry. I didn't mean to pry," Jules said uncomfortably.

Joe was angry now and was getting worked up remembering his ex-wife.

"She never shut up! It was always something. 'Joe, don't forget to pick your socks up off the floor.' 'Joe, can you mow the lawn this weekend?' 'Joe, can you pick up some tampons for me at the drugstore?'...She was such a nag!" Joe halfway yelled in anger.

Jules was really uncomfortable now and she started to look around for the moderator to ring the bell. She couldn't wait to move on from this loser. To her relief, the bell then rang.

"Okay, time's up," the moderator said into a microphone up at a podium. "Gentlemen, please stand and rotate one spot to your left. Ladies, please remain seated," the moderator instructed. "And now, you'll have another five minutes to talk to your next date," the moderator stated.

"Well Joe, it was interesting meeting you," Jules said. Joe was in his own world now, still thinking about his ex-wife.

"Nag, nag, nag!" he said as he got up and moved one spot over to his left just in time for some new guy to sit down in his place.

Jules immediately perked up when she saw the new guy that was sitting down across from her. He was about six feet tall, he was stylishly dressed in a cable-knit sweater and slacks, and he had the cutest dimples when he flashed his megawatt smile at Jules.

"Well, hi there!" the new guy said enthusiastically.

"Well, hi yourself!" Jules replied just as excited, as she reached out her hand to shake his.

"I'm Ashe, and you are...?" the new guy inquired still holding onto Jules' hand.

"Jules. It's nice to meet you Ashe," she answered still smiling, as Ashe finally let her hand go.

"So, what's a pretty lady like you doing at a speed dating party?" Ashe asked.

"Well, I thought that it might be a nice way to meet new people," she answered as if she were on a job interview.

"Yeah, that's why I came too. I almost didn't come, but a buddy of mine convinced me to give it a try," Ashe offered.

"So this is your first time coming to one of these then?" Jules asked feeling relieved to be talking to someone seemingly normal.

"Yeah. A friend of mine met his wife at one of these dating parties, so he suggested that I come," Ashe responded.

"Why, are you looking for a wife?" Jules asked, trying not to be obvious that she was thinking of him as an exciting prospect.

"Well, not actively. But if the right woman came along, I'd certainly be open to marriage," Ashe answered honestly. "You know, I'm surprised that some lucky guy hasn't snatched an attractive woman like you up by now."

"Well, I came close once, but it didn't work out. I guess I haven't met the right guy yet," she answered openly.

"Same with me. I just haven't found that special connection with any of the women that I've dated," he agreed.

Their eyes met for a few seconds and they both blushed. Jules noticed those dimples again. Ashe was definitely a cutie. It seemed like they were having a moment where they both realized that there was an attraction there.

"So Ashe, what do you do for a living?" Jules asked.

"I work in healthcare," Ashe answered.

"That's a very noble and important industry," Jules said.

"Thanks. It's pretty rewarding getting to help people every day," he responded. He was liking Jules more and more. "But let's not spend too much time talking about work. You're the first woman that I've met here tonight that I've enjoyed talking to, and I hate that the bell is gonna go off at any second."

"I know. It is a bit nerve-wracking. But look, in case we run out of time, here's my card," Jules said as she reached into her purse, pulled out her business card, and handed it to him. "Maybe we can meet for coffee sometime so we can talk for more than just five minutes and not feel so rushed."

"Thanks. I'd like that. I'd like that very much," Ashe said smiling with those adorable dimples, as he took the card from Jules over the table.

"Well, since the bell hasn't gone off yet, why don't you tell me what you're looking for in a woman?" Jules asked.

"Let's see. I'd like her to be attractive, and smart, and to have a great sense of humor. And it's really important that she's easy to talk to," Ashe answered.

Just then, the bell rang.

"Oh no! Our time's up," Jules said disappointed.

"Well, I have your card. I'll give you a call so we can grab that coffee and get to know each other better," Ashe said charmingly.

"That would be nice. I look forward to it," Jules responded smiling.

Ashe got up and moved to the left as another guy sat down in front of Jules. She snuck a peak at Ashe one last time before she turned her attention to the new guy that was now sitting in front of her.

***

A few evenings later, Jules was just getting home from work when her cell phone rang.

"Hello?" Jules answered. She smiled when she heard Ashe's voice on the other end. She pushed the speaker phone button on her phone so she could talk to him while she got settled in at home.

"Yes, hi Ashe. Of course I remember meeting you," Jules answered, hoping that he couldn't hear just how much she was smiling.

"Well, there were so many people at the speed dating party the other night that I didn't want to take it for granted that you remembered meeting me," he said modestly.

"How could I forget those dimples?" Jules said flirtatiously, and they both laughed.

"So listen," he started "I know that we said that we'd go out for coffee, but I'd love to take you to dinner if you're interested."

Jules' smile widened even more. She did a little happy dance around her living room.

"Uh, sure. Dinner sounds great," she said trying to play it cool.

"Okay great. Are you free tomorrow night?" Ashe asked.

"Sure. I can move some things around to make myself available," she said coyly trying not to sound too excited. She plopped down onto her couch and kicked her sneakers off.

"Fantastic! I'd love to take you to my favorite spot. You're not a vegetarian are you?" he inquired.

"Nope. I love meat, fish, the whole shebang," She answered still smiling.

"Awesome. This spot is close to my house, so do you mind meeting me there?" he asked.

"Um. Sure, I can do that," she answered, a little disappointed that he wasn't planning to pick her up. But, she guessed that meeting up for a first date wasn't the worse thing in the world.

"Do you have a pen and paper? I'll give you the address," he said.

"Sure, hold on a sec while I grab a Post-It and a pen," she said as she ran into her bedroom to the desk that sat against the wall. She opened the desk drawer and pulled out a Post-It pad and a pen. "Okay, I'm ready."

She'd taken him off of speaker phone, as she scribbled down the address onto the pad.

"I look forward to seeing you tomorrow night too," she said into the phone as she listened to his response.

"Okay, goodnight," she said as she hung up. She spun around in excitement and fell onto her bed giddily. Tomorrow night, she could be having her first date with her future husband!

***

The next evening, after work, Jules walked up the stairs from the subway. Immediately, she wasn't crazy about the neighborhood. The address that Ashe had given her was in a bit of a seedy area. Jules instinctively reached into her purse for her pepper spray, and she put it in her suit jacket pocket for protection.

She walked about two blocks to the address that Ashe had given her, and stopped in front of a rundown looking grocery store. This couldn't be it.

She pulled out the Post-It to double-check that she'd scribbled down the right address. The address on the Post-It matched the address of the grocery store.

"Damn, did I write down the wrong address?" Jules said to herself.

Just as she pulled out her cell phone to call Ashe, Jules saw him running up the sidewalk from a block away.

"Hey! Jules, you made it. Sorry, I'm a little late," he said a bit out of breath. He was dressed in blue hospital scrubs, like he had just walked out of an operating room.

"No worries," Jules responded as Ashe stopped in front of her. "I was just about to call you. I must've written the wrong address down," she said, showing him her Post-It. "The address that I wrote down is for this grocery store."

"No, you got it right," he said smiling at her.

"But, this is a grocery store," she said not understanding. "You said that you were taking me to one of your favorite spots."

"Yeah, this store is one of my favorite spots. They have the best meat selection in town," he said.

"Oh okay, I get it. You're trying to see if I have a sense of humor," she laughed. "Ha ha, very funny. So where's the restaurant? Around the corner?" she asked waiting for the punch line to what definitely had to be a joke.

"No, I'm serious," he said. "I don't believe in taking dates to restaurants. It's just so pretentious. And you spend all of this money to eat some tiny portion of food, just so they can stick you with a big bill at the end. It's so annoying."

"Are you serious?" Jules asked incredulously, her smile fading. "You're taking me to a grocery store for our dinner date?"

"Yes, I'm serious. Come on, don't knock it until you've tried it. The food is good, and it's cheap," he said as he opened the door to the grocery store and held it for Jules to walk in.

She walked into the store in amazement that this guy actually thought that this was a cool date. He led her down one of the aisles to the back of the store, and walked her up to the meat counter.

"Pick your meat," he said proudly. "You can have any meat you want. It's on me."

"Seriously?" Jules asked, surprised that this wasn't a joke after all. Did Mr. Dimples actually just say "Pick your meat" with a straight face? Like he was some big spender that was treating her to a fine dining experience? Jules prided herself on not being a snob, but come on! This was ridiculous! It was starting to set in that this was about to become one of the worst dates that she'd ever been on.

The butcher walked up to the counter when he saw that he had customers.

"What can I get for you?" the butcher asked nonchalantly, like he asked that question one hundred times a day.

"Go on," Ashe urged with a smile. "I'm gonna make you the best sandwich that you've ever had," he said proudly.

"Umm," Jules hesitated, trying to process this whole situation. "Can I get the roast beef?" Jules asked slowly to the butcher. Was she really ordering lunch meat for her dinner date?

"Actually, the turkey is better," Ashe interrupted. "And it's fifty cents cheaper per pound."

Oh my God! This was the cheapest guy that Jules had ever met! Wow!

"Okay, give me the turkey then," Jules said. This was pathetic.

"And how much do you want?" the butcher asked.

"I guess give me a pound," Jules answered. Not sure what the hell she was going to do with a pound of turkey after this nightmare date was over.

"A pound?" Ashe said to Jules in disbelief. "Are you crazy? Do you know how much a pound of turkey costs? Besides, a petite woman like you can't eat a pound of meat."

"Okay," Jules responded to Ashe holding her tongue. This was actually becoming comical.

"Just give me a half pound of the turkey please," she told the butcher.

"Yup. Got it," the butcher said to Jules. "And for you sir?" he asked Ashe.

"Yeah, just give me a half pound of the honey baked ham," Ashe said to the butcher.

Jules was starting to laugh in her mind thinking about how much her friends were going to crack up when she told them about this date. So she decided to have some fun with the notoriously cheap Ashe.

"So, can I get some cheese to go with that sandwich, or would that be asking for too much?" she asked half teasing Ashe.

"Okay, if you must," he answered, not realizing that Jules was being facetious.

"Can you throw in a quarter pound of provolone please?" Jules yelled out to the butcher who was already slicing the turkey that she'd ordered.

"Sure. No problem," the butcher responded.

Jules realized that she was going to have to get an exit strategy in place quickly to get her out of this disaster of a date. While the butcher got their orders together, Jules thought of an idea.

"I'm gonna go find some chips to go with this yummy sandwich that you're making me. I'll be right back," she said to Ashe as she walked away. As soon as she was out of Ashe's sight, she ducked into the potato chips aisle and pulled out her cell phone. She started texting quickly.

> *Hey Charlie, I'm on the date from hell! PLEASE HELP!!! Call me on my cell ASAP. Thx!*

Then she grabbed a bag of Lays potato chips and walked back out to the meat counter, where the butcher was handing Ashe three packages wrapped in white deli paper.

"Oh there you are," he said cheerfully to Jules when she walked up with a bag of chips. "We're all set."

"Well what about bread and mayo?" Jules asked trying to stall to give Charlie time to see her text.

"Oh I've got that back at my house," he said as he walked towards the front of the store.

"We're going back to your house?" she asked incredulously. Did he really think that she was clueless enough to go back to his house with him? There was no way in hell that was happening. If Charlie didn't call soon, then she'd have to think of another way to get out of this date.

Ashe and Jules walked up to the cashier, where Ashe reached into his back pocket for his wallet. The cashier rang up the meat, cheese and chips.

"That'll be $23.47." the cashier said. Ashe opened his wallet and pulled out $15.

"Hey, do you have $9?" he asked Jules. "I wasn't expecting you to go running up the bill with your cheese and potato chips, so I don't have enough to cover it," he smiled at Jules, revealing dimples that were no longer appealing. How did a guy, who seemed so normal when she met him, turn out to be such a character?

Jules could not believe that this fool just asked her to pay for part of this grocery store sham of a date. This was definitely going down in the history books as Worst Date Ever! She reached into her purse and pulled out her Gucci wallet. She opened the wallet and handed a ten dollar bill to Ashe.

Just then, as if there was an angel watching out for her, Jules' cell phone rang from inside of her purse. Yes! She was about to get out of this crazy situation that she'd gotten herself into.

"Hey Charlie," she answered after pulling the phone out of her purse. She was so relieved to hear his voice.

"What? How did it get deleted?" she asked into the phone in a pretend conversation. "You've gotta be kidding me… But I've already left the office… Alright fine, I'll come back in… I'll see you in about a half hour… Thanks. Bye," Jules said into the phone and hung up.

She turned to Ashe, who had finished paying the cashier, and was standing behind Jules with a plastic bag.

"You're not going to believe this," she started. "I've got an important meeting tomorrow morning, and a motion that I wrote for it somehow got deleted. I'm sorry but I'm going to have to cut our date short and head back to the office to rewrite the damn thing," she explained, faking disappointment.

"Oh no. That sucks," he said. "I was really having a good time."

"Yeah well, I guess a lawyer's work is never done," Jules joked. "Thanks for the date. Sorry I had to cut out early."

"Don't worry about it. We can do it again some other time. I'll give you a call," he yelled out as Jules quickly walked away. That was a phone call that

Jules would never ever pick up, Jules thought to herself.

She walked back up the street to the subway station, relieved that her night of insanity was over. She owed Charlie big time for this one.

***

The next morning, Jules walked up the steps from the subway station below. She walked quickly down the street as if she was in a hurry. She pulled out her cell phone and speed dialed her office.

"Hey Phyllis, it's me," Jules said while walking. "Any messages?... Okay, I'll give her a call when I get into the office. I'll be in at around eleven since I have my annual check-up this morning... Okay thanks."

Jules put the cell phone back into her purse and walked quickly into a building.

***

A few minutes later, Jules was sitting in an examination room on the exam table in a hospital gown. She was flipping through a People magazine as she waited for Dr. Marshall, her gynecologist. Just then, Dr. Marshall walked in. She was in her mid-50s and had a bad habit of speaking her mind.

"Well hello Miss Alexander," Dr. Marshall said as she walked into the examination room.

"Hi Dr. Marshall," Jules said almost as if she was back in high school and the teacher had just walked into the classroom.

"And how is one of my favorite patients doing?" asked Dr. Marshall while looking at Jules' chart.

"Oh I'm fine. Just been busy with work," Jules answered.

"I see that you're here for your annual physical," Dr. Marshall stated still reviewing Jules' chart.

"Uh huh," Jules answered. She hated going to the gynecologist. As important as it is to keep up with annual physicals, it always felt like such a violation of her body.

"Well, let's get you up in the stirrups," Dr. Marshall instructed.

Jules laid back on the examination table and put her feet into the stirrups that were attached to the end of the table. She really hated this part of the exam, but she knew that millions of women went through this every day to stay healthy, so she would suck it up and do the same.

She began staring at a picture of a tropical beach that was taped to the ceiling directly above the exam table. I guess Dr. Marshall had put the picture there so her patients would have something to stare at while their insides were being poked and prodded. Jules began to stare at the beach in the picture as if she was willing herself to be miraculously transported there.

Jules started to breathe in and out of her mouth slowly as she laid on her back, as if she was trying to stay calm. Her feet were firmly planted in the stirrups while her legs were spread wide in the air to give the doctor easy access.

"Okay Jules, you know the procedure. I'm just going to do a pap smear, take some cultures, check your uterus and then we'll be all done," Dr. Marshall said reassuringly.

"Okay," Jules managed to say.

"So, how's your love life Miss Alexander. Are you seeing anyone special?" Dr. Marshall asked while she conducted the pelvic exam.

"Nope," Jules said a little annoyed and breathless since she was still breathing in and out of her mouth during the exam. Frankly, she didn't think that this was an appropriate topic of discussion while the good doctor had her hand up Jules' cooch.

"Well, what are you waiting for honey? You're running out of time you know. At your age, your biological window will be closing in a few years. And if you want to have more than one child, you're going to have to get started soon," Dr. Marshall advised.

Jules couldn't believe that she was being lectured about still being single while she was spread eagle up in the stirrups. As if she didn't feel vulnerable enough! Could this exam be over already?

"Well, I have a very demanding job," Jules said quickly trying to get back to her rhythmic breathing.

"Uh huh. Look, do you want to have a kid or not?" Dr. Marshall pressed on.

"Of course I do! Someday," Jules said a little louder than she'd wanted, but she was starting to get angry. She forced herself to look up at the beach on the ceiling again to try to calm back down.

"Then you're going to have to work less on the job and work more on finding a husband," Dr. Marshall continued on, oblivious to how uncomfortable she was making her patient. She was like a dog with a bone trying to make her point.

"What do you want me to do Doctor? Go pick up some random guy off the street and let him knock me up?" Jules said with an attitude. She was angry now that Dr. Marshall was being so insensitive and unprofessional.

Dr. Marshall stopped her pelvic exam for a few seconds and shot Jules a look, like the look that mothers give their kids to warn them to stop misbehaving.

Jules knew that look and took a breath to calm back down again.

"Lately I've been trying to date, but it's hard to find that special connection with someone," Jules said a little calmer. She wished this interrogation could be over already.

"You keep trying then. And don't let these fast-talking men talk you into having unprotected sex with them. There are so many diseases out there nowadays," Dr. Marshall proclaimed as if she was Jules' mother and not a healthcare professional.

"Well, I've been celibate for over a year," Jules responded, halfway relieved that she'd had absolutely no love life recently.

"Yes, but now that you're getting back out there and dating again, don't let these slicksters con you into bed. Men are dogs. You just keep your legs closed until you find a really good man to put a ring on it," Dr. Marshall said, on a roll now.

Just then, there was a knock at the door.

"Yes, come in," Dr. Marshall yelled out while she had her hand up in Jules' uterus.

Jules heard the door open and couldn't believe that Dr. Marshall had just told someone to come in while she was all exposed. Because her knees were in the way, Jules couldn't see who had just walked into the exam room.

"Sorry, to interrupt, but Doctor your daughter is on the phone," a male voice said. The voice sounded familiar to Jules, so she moved one of her knees to see who the voice belonged to.

"Oh my God!" Jules shrieked when she saw that the male voice belonged to Ashe. Jules was starting to think that she was being punished for something she'd done in a past life.

"Oh wow. Hey Jules!" Ashe said excited to see her again, it not registering that all of her private business was right in front of him. "I didn't realize when I saw 'Julia Alexander' on the schedule today that that was you."

"Wait, you two know each other?" Dr. Marshall interrupted.

"Doctor, remember when I told you that I went out on a date with this cool chick last night?" he asked.

"I cannot believe that this is happening?" Jules said to herself, beyond embarrassed since she was still up in the stirrups with the doctor's hand still inside of her.

"No way! This is the girl you were just raving about this morning?" Dr. Marshall asked excitedly.

"Someone just shoot me now!" Jules said to herself.

"Yep, this is the girl. Talk about a small world," Ashe said. "Jules, this works out perfectly. You saved me a phone call. So, you owe me a make-up date from last night. What's a good day for you?"

"Seriously?" Jules couldn't believe that this guy was asking her out on a second date while she was half naked in an examination room. "I don't exactly have my calendar in front of me Ashe." she said sarcastically.

"Well look, you two lovebirds can talk after I finish here," Dr. Marshall interrupted. "Ashe, please tell my daughter I'll call her back."

"Okay, will do Doctor," Ashe answered dutifully. "Jules, I'll catch up with you after your appointment."

"Yeah. Swell." Jules answered sarcastically, as Ashe walked back out of the exam room.

After her pelvic exam from hell, Jules was signing some paperwork as Ashe walked up. He seemed ecstatic to see her again.

"Hey, can you believe this coincidence?" he asked completely clueless that Jules didn't seem as happy to see him.

"Honestly, I'm horrified beyond belief!" Jules whispered loudly, hoping that the receptionist couldn't hear them talking.

"Horrified, why?" Ashe asked not getting it.

"Please tell me you're kidding," Jules said wishing she could just run for the door and never see this guy again. Ashe just stood there looking confused.

"We only had one date, if you want to call it that, and then this morning, you got to see... EVERYTHING!" Jules said trying to keep her voice down.

"Jules, I'm a nurse. I've seen it all before. You have nothing to feel embarrassed about," Ashe said trying to reassure her.

"Well you haven't seen MINE before!" she said still loud whispering.

"Come on. You don't have to be squeamish with me," he said. "Look, I'm on a break right now. Do you have time to grab a quick cup of coffee with me? I'm buying."

"Uh, no. I'm sorry. I have to get to work," Jules said quickly as she started inching her way towards the exit door.

"Oh. Okay. Well, when's a good time to call you?" Ashe asked.

"Um, I'm thinking never. This whole thing has been a bit traumatic for me Ashe," Jules said honestly. She had absolutely no intention of ever going out on another date with him again after the grocery store debacle, and now this ultra-humiliating experience.

Then, Jules walked out of the doctor's office, leaving poor Ashe standing there. Jules walked to the elevators lost in thought.

"Oh well. Back to the drawing board," Jules mumbled to herself as she stepped into the elevator. She pulled her cell phone out of her purse and pushed the record button.

"Reminder to self – Find a new gynecologist," Jules said into her phone as the elevator doors closed.

CHAPTER 5

Thursday evening, Jules was back at her office working at her desk. She was wearing reading glasses and writing notes on a legal pad, when her phone buzzed. Jules stopped writing and clicked a button on her phone.

"Yes Phyllis?" Jules called out.

"Mylyn is on the phone for you," Phyllis' voice responded through the speaker phone.

"Okay, put her through please," Jules answered.

Jules' phone rang and she picked it up.

"Hey lady... I know, we've been playing phone tag... Yes, I know. I still can't believe you and Andrew are tying the knot in six weeks... Uh huh... Uh huh... Okay, I'll come with you, Robin and Maggie on Saturday. We can pick out our dresses then... Alright girl. You hang in there... I know planning a wedding in such a short time must be driving you nuts… Totally. I'll help you in any way that I can... Okay sweetie. Bye," and Jules hung up.

After a few seconds, Jules' phone buzzed again. Jules touched the button on her phone.

"Yes Phyllis?" Jules called out.

"Hey, you wanted me to remind you that you have to leave at 6:45 to meet Robin's cousin at the theatre," Phyllis' voice said over the speaker phone.

"Oh that's right. Thanks for the reminder. By the way, did you see Charlie today?" Jules asked.

"No, he called in sick," Phyllis' voice responded.

"He did? Oh. Okay, thanks," Jules said before she hung up the speaker phone.

She sat for a minute thinking about Charlie calling in sick. She picked up the phone and dialed his number. While she was waiting for Charlie to answer the phone, Jules began to pack up for the day. She got his voicemail, so Jules left him a message.

Hey Charlie, it's me. You didn't come to work today so I just wanted to call to check on you.

Hopefully you're not really sick and you were just playing hooky. Hope you did something fun on your day off. I'm leaving work now, but I'll catch up with you tomorrow. Give me a call if you need anything. Okay, bye.

Then Jules pulled the compact out of her desk, and checked her hair and make-up. She looked out the window and noticed that it was raining pretty hard. She then grabbed a red umbrella out of her desk, along with her purse and briefcase, and walked out of the office on her way to her blind date with Robin's cousin.

***

About an hour later, it was raining pretty hard outside of the Majestic Theatre in the Broadway district. Robin's cousin was taking Jules to see "The Phantom of the Opera", one of Jules' favorite musicals of all time. There were several people staying dry under an underpass in front of the theatre as they waited for their theatre companions to arrive.

Jules got out of an Uber with her umbrella raised, and ran to the underpass to stay dry with the other theatre goers. She had just begun to shake out her wet umbrella when Mr. Chase Wilder walked up to her.

He was six foot one, appeared to have an athletic build under his very expensive suit, and had movie star looks that could easily land him on the cover of GQ Magazine. Robin had told Jules that Chase was forty-five years old, but Jules wouldn't have thought that he was a day over thirty-five. Jules had only seen him a few seconds ago, but she was attracted to him immediately.

"Jules, is that you?" Chase asked in a deep masculine voice.

"Hi. Yes. Chase?" Jules asked in return.

"Yes, hi. I have to say, you're even more breathtaking than your Facebook profile picture. It's great to finally meet you," he said to Jules as he reached out his hand. They shook hands, both smiling approvingly at each other.

"It's great to meet you too! Robin has been telling me that we should meet for some time now, so I'm glad that we finally connected," Jules said trying to regain her composure and sound like she had some sense.

"Yes, I agree," Chase said gazing into Jules' eyes. "Hey, let's get you out of this rain."

Chase, being a gentleman, opened the theatre door and held it open for Jules. They walked through the lobby of the theatre to a bar lounge where there were a number of theatre patrons mingling amongst themselves before the show was set to begin.

"Can I get you anything from the bar?" he asked.

"Sure. I'll take a seltzer with lime please," she said, impressed with his suave style.

Chase walked off towards the bar as Jules checked him out from behind, clearly impressed with what she was seeing.

"Things are definitely looking up," Jules mumbled to herself giddily.

After a couple of minutes, Chase returned with Jules' seltzer and a bottle of water for himself.

"One seltzer and lime for the lady," he said in a mock British accent, handing the glass to Jules.

"Why thank you kind sir," Jules responded in her own fake British accent with a smile. "So, why haven't I met you before now? I thought that I'd met all of Robin's family."

"Well, I just moved to New York from Chicago a month ago. I relocated my business here."

"Oh, and what business are you in?" Jules asked, as if she hadn't already grilled Robin for every detail about her cousin before Jules would agree to go out with him.

"I manage a hedge fund," he replied modestly.

"Wow. That's impressive. I've always been a bit intimidated by high finance," Jules offered.

"I find that hard to believe. Robin told me that you have an MBA as well as a JD. You're pretty impressive yourself," Chase complimented.

"Well, thank you. But my MBA was in Marketing. I was too chicken to tackle the super complicated world of Finance like my classmates that went on to become investment bankers," Jules said downplaying her time at Columbia Business School.

"Well, I think that you're probably being modest. I get the sense that you could do anything that you put your mind to," Chase said.

Jules and Chase had a moment where they just stood in the lounge looking at each other smiling, each pleased with their date. There was definitely a mutual attraction. Then, the overhead lights flickered.

"Uh, we'd better get to our seats since the show is about to start," Chase said breaking the brief spell that he and Jules had been in.

"Yes, you're right," Jules responded coming back to Earth as they put their drinks down on a cocktail table.

"Milady," Chase said as he stuck out his arm as if offering to escort Jules into the theatre. Jules smiled, slid her arm into his, and they walked out of the lounge to go take their seats.

***

After the show, Jules and Chase were sitting at a table in a restaurant. They seemed to really be enjoying each other's company as they dined on a couple of desserts.

"Thanks again for inviting me out tonight. 'Phantom of the Opera' has always been one of my favorite shows. The music is so beautiful and emotional," Jules said.

"It's one of my favorites too. I've seen it six times so far. Does that sound crazy?" Chase asked.

"Well, not to me since tonight was my eighth time seeing that show," Jules said, and they both laughed.

"The music and the story line is some powerful stuff," Chase said.

"I know. It's beautiful and sad at the same time. And the loneliness that the Phantom felt his whole life... it breaks my heart every time," Jules said thoughtfully as if she was back at the theatre reliving the show.

"Speaking of which, did I see you shed a tear or two at the end?" Chase teased.

"You saw that, huh? I thought that I'd done a better job of hiding it," Jules laughed.

"You don't have to hide tears from me," Chase said thoughtfully.

"I couldn't help it. When Christine kissed the Phantom at the end to save her fiancé, it hit me that this was the first time that anyone had ever gotten that close to him. No one had ever kissed him or held him before. He'd never experienced love or affection. It was just so sad," Jules said, feeling a little emotional and starting to get choked up again.

"See, I'm a mess. That show gets me every time!" Jules joked trying to lighten the mood.

"I can see that. You really felt his pain," Chase said observing Jules' compassionate heart.

"I guess I could relate to him on some level," Jules offered.

"Oh yeah? In what way?" Chase asked leaning forward, as if he was hanging on every word.

"Well, I broke off an engagement about a year ago, and I haven't gotten involved with anyone seriously since," Jules confessed.

"I see," Chase said as he continued to listen.

"There were definitely times when I thought that I'd die from the loneliness," Jules said remembering her tough year.

"I know what you mean. When my marriage broke up two years ago, I didn't know how I was going to get through it," he said honestly.

"I'm sorry," Jules said supportively.

"Thank you," Chase responded sincerely.

"But we made it through, right?" Jules said trying to cheer the mood back up. "So, no more gloom and doom talk. Let's talk about something more positive."

"Yeah, like these amazing desserts. How was your tiramisu?" he asked perking back up again.

"It's absolutely sinful. Do you wanna try some?" she asked as if they'd shared many desserts before tonight.

"Absolutely! My mama didn't raise me to turn down good food from a beautiful woman," he joked flirtatiously.

Jules took Chase's fork, scooped up a forkful of her tiramisu, and handed the fork back to him. He put the fork into his mouth, and closed his eyes to savor the delicious dessert.

"Whooee! Damn, girl! That's good! I'm a total foodie, so I'm in Heaven right now!" Chase exclaimed. "Okay, now you're gonna have to try some of my chocolate lava cake. It's still warm, so the chocolate is still melted," Chase said as he reached across the table and picked up Jules' fork.

"Definitely. It looks amazing," Jules said excitedly.

Chase scooped up a big forkful of the chocolate lava cake. Then, he reached across the table and fed the cake to Jules.

"Oh my God! That's sinful! Wow! That may be one of the best chocolate lava cakes that I've ever tasted," Jules said with a mouth full of cake. She was having such an amazing evening with Mr. Chase Wilder.

***

Later, a black Chevy Suburban pulled up outside of Jules' apartment building. A well-dressed chauffer got out of the driver's side and walked to the back of the SUV. He opened the back door, and Chase climbed out. Then, Chase held his hand out to Jules to help her out of the back seat, and they walked into her building.

Moments later, Jules and Chase got off of the elevator on Jules' floor, and walked down the hall to Jules' apartment. Once in front of Jules' door, they stopped walking, and Jules turned around to face her date.

"Chase, I had a really great time tonight," Jules said.

"Me too. I hope that you'll let me take you out again sometime," Chase said not trying to sound too cocky.

"I'd like that," Jules responded.

All of a sudden, there was an awkward silence. The kind of silence that happens on a first date, where both parties are trying to figure out if there should be a kiss goodnight.

"Are you feeling as nervous as I am right now?" Chase asked trying to break the awkwardness.

"Yes. Why, does it show?" Jules answered, relieved that she wasn't the only one feeling nervous.

"No. Not at all. I was just hoping that I wasn't the only one with a few butterflies banging around my stomach right now," Chase said with a nervous laugh. He really liked this woman and he didn't want to blow it by moving too fast.

"No, I've got them too. What are you so nervous about anyway?" Jules asked, as if she didn't already know the answer.

"I'm wondering if it would be okay if I kissed you goodnight," Chase said, taking a chance.

"I think that I'd be a little disappointed if you didn't," Jules said boldly.

Then, Jules used Chase's tie to pull him towards her into a kiss. He was pleasantly surprised at her willingness to make the first move. Their lips touched lightly at first. Then, Chase pulled Jules in closer into a deeper kiss, and Jules happily matched his intensity.

Jules' arms were wrapped around Chase's neck as they hungrily kissed in front of her door. The electricity was so powerful, and Jules didn't want the moment to end. Just then, Chase pulled back. He knew that he would enjoy kissing Jules all night long, but he really wanted to take his time with her.

"Wow," Jules said breathlessly, still in Chase's arms.

"I know. Wow!" Chase said starting to kiss Jules with gentle light kisses. Feeling himself getting caught up again, he pulled back.

"I should go," Chase said.

"Yeah," Jules said back. She wished he would stay, but she knew that it was best that he go.

"Unless you want me to stay," Chase said, losing his resolve not to sleep with Jules on the first date.

"Of course I want you to stay," Jules said almost in a whisper. "And that's why you should go," she said with a sexy smile.

"You're right," Chase said as he kissed Jules on the forehead. "Jules Alexander! I'll have to get on my cousin for not introducing us years ago."

"Well, I guess timing is everything," Jules responded.

"So true. I'll give you a call tomorrow," Chase said.

"Okay," Jules said wishing that he could stay.

Jules pulled her keys from her purse and opened her door. She walked in slowly and turned around.

"Thanks again for a fun date," she said.

"No. Thank you," Chase replied.

"Goodnight," Jules said smiling.

"Sweet dreams," Chase responded, half wishing that Jules would insist that he come inside.

But instead, Jules slowly closed the door. She leaned back on the door and touched her lips as if she was reliving that amazing kiss. Then, she ran over to her couch and threw herself onto it giddily. She grabbed a pillow and covered her face, while she stomped her feet on the couch excitedly.

"Yes, yes, yes! Thank you God!" she yelled in a muffled voice from under the pillow.

***

The next morning at work, Jules walked down the hallway with a big, glowing smile. She was about to walk into her office when Phyllis stopped her.

"I see someone had a good time last night," Phyllis stated.

"I don't know what you mean," Jules replied playfully.

"Well first, you've got this huge grin on your face," Phyllis observed.

"Do I?" Jules responded. She couldn't stop smiling.

"Uh huh! And second... Well, you'll see what I mean in a minute. Robin's cousin must've been one hot date!" Phyllis hinted.

"Oh Phyllis, you're such a gossip," Jules teased.

Just then, Jules opened her office door and was shocked to find that her office was filled with bouquets and bouquets of red long-stemmed roses.

"What the...?" was all that Jules managed to say.

"They arrived about a half hour ago," Phyllis said, as she excitedly walked up behind Jules.

Jules walked over to one of twenty-something bouquets and picked out a card.

She began to read the card out loud:

Beautiful Jules,
Thank you for an incredible first date. I can't wait to see you

again. Hopefully, you're free this evening. There's a special place that I'd like to take you to. I'll give you a call later.

Thinking of you,
Chase

"Ooh la la! You hooked a live one!" Phyllis swooned as she walked back to her desk.

"Good looking, smart and romantic? Could he be the one?" Jules wondered to herself.

***

A few minutes later, Charlie stepped off of the elevator at work. All alone in the hallway, he took a small black velvet box out of his pants pocket. He opened the box to marvel at the stunning diamond solitaire engagement ring that was inside. He smiled, closed the box and put it back into his pocket.

Then, he walked cheerfully down the hallway towards his office. But, when he overheard Phyllis and Jules marveling over something in Jules' office, he made a detour and stopped outside of Jules' office instead.

"Hey, what are all of the "ooh's" and "aah's" about?" he asked in a chipper mood.

Just then, Charlie saw all of the roses in Jules' office.

"Damn, who died?" Charlie asked jokingly.

"They're from Jules' new beau," gossipy Phyllis said as she went back to her desk. She just couldn't help herself.

"What new beau?" Charlie asked not worried about any real competition. "Oh right, was it one of those jokers from the other night at Luke's?"

"No. Actually, these are from Chase, Robin's cousin," Jules explained. "Remember, Robin set me up on a blind date with him? Well, we had our first date last night."

"What do you mean first date? Are you saying that there's gonna be a second date?" Charlie asked starting to get worried as he began to notice how excited Jules seemed to be over this Chase guy.

"Yes Charlie. There's going to be a second date, and probably a third and a forth, and maybe a lot more dates after that," Jules said dreamily. "Charlie, I think that he might be The One!"

Charlie felt his heart sink. He tried to control his anger, but he was losing his patience.

"Come on, after one date and a mausoleum of flowers, you think that you're ready to marry this clown?" he argued.

"How can you call him a clown? You haven't even met him," Jules said starting to get annoyed.

"Look, anyone that sends this many flowers after just one date is either a player or is over-compensating for something. Either way he's a clown," Charlie said sarcastically.

"You know, I really don't get you! You've been in such a foul mood lately. As my friend, why can't you just be happy for me?" Jules asked frustrated.

"As your friend? You see, that's the problem right there!" Charlie yelled.

"Now you've really lost me," Jules responded.

"Oh never mind!" Charlie said exasperated and started to leave.

"Hey, don't go. You never told me what you ended up doing on your day off yesterday," Jules said trying to calm Charlie down.

"Oh nothing. Just wasted a lot of time," Charlie said as he fidgeted around with the ring box in his pants pocket. Then, he stormed out of Jules' office.

Before Jules had too much time to wonder about what was upsetting Charlie, her phone buzzed. She walked over to her desk phone and pushed a button.

"Yes Phyllis?" Jules called out.

"Chase Wilder is on the line!" Phyllis' voice said giddily over the speaker phone.

"Thanks Phyllis. Put him through please," Jules said with a big grin.

Jules' phone rang.

"Well hello there... Yes, I saw them about five minutes ago. They're absolutely gorgeous. Thank you!... Of course I like them. I love them! But you shouldn't have gone through so much trouble... Aww, that's sweet... Okay I'm listening... Yes, I'm free tonight... Uh, yes I think I can be downstairs at 6:30. Why, what are you up to Mr. Wilder?... A surprise huh?... Okay, no more questions. I'll see you tonight... me too. Bye."

Jules took one of the roses out of the bouquet that was sitting on her desk. She smelled it as she gazed out the window. She started daydreaming about Mr. Chase Wilder.

***

Later that evening, there was a silver and black Rolls-Royce Phantom parked in front of Jules' office building. Jules walked outside with Phyllis in tow behind her since Phyllis was dying to meet the wonderful Chase Wilder. When Jules spotted Chase leaning against the Rolls holding a red rose, she stopped walking, stunned in amazement.

"Oh - my - God!" was all that she managed to say.

Phyllis looked around anxiously to see what had stopped her boss in her tracks.

"Oh wow! Is that him?" Phyllis asked, impressed with Chase's good looks, sharp suit, and of course, the Rolls. This man was the whole package.

"Yep, that's him," Jules said, trying to regain her composure. Still shocked, she walked slowly up to Chase, smiling from ear to ear.

"So, this is how you impress a girl? It's pretty shabby Mr. Wilder," Jules joked flirtatiously.

"Oh damn. I guess I'll need to up my game then," Chase said flirting back with Jules as he leaned in to give her a quick kiss on the cheek. Then, he noticed a grinning Phyllis hiding behind Jules.

"And who is this lovely lady?" he asked. Phyllis blushed like a school girl.

"Oh, I'm sorry. This is my assistant, Phyllis," Jules said. "Phyllis Shelton, this is Chase Wilder."

"It's a pleasure to meet you Phyllis," Chase said as he held out his hand.

"The pleasure is all mine," Phyllis responded grinning as she shook Chase's hand.

Jules shook her head trying not to laugh, as she watched her assistant acting like a complete goofball.

"Your chariot awaits Mademoiselle," Chase said charmingly as he turned his attention back to Jules. "A beautiful rose for a beautiful lady," he said as he handed Jules the rose.

Just then, Tony, Chase's well-dressed driver, got out of the driver's side, walked around, and opened the back door.

"By the way, I forgot to introduce you to my driver, Tony, last night," Chase said charmingly. "Jules this is Tony. He's been taking great care of me since I moved to New York last month."

"It's a pleasure to meet you Ma'am," a smiling Tony said to Jules as he continued to hold the door open.

"Thanks Tony! It's nice to meet you too," Jules replied, as Chase took her hand. He led her into the back of the Rolls, and climbed in after her. Jules felt like she had just walked into a fairytale as she sat down on the super soft cream colored leather seats.

Phyllis was watching from a few feet away admiring Mr. Chase Wilder' style.

"You go girl!" she yelled, as the Rolls pulled away from the curb.

"Damn, I've gotta get me one of him!" she said to herself as she walked back towards the office building.

Inside the Rolls, Jules was sitting next to Chase as Tony drove them through Midtown.

"Chase, you are unbelievable! I cannot believe that you showed up at my job in this car!" Jules said incredulously. "Who does that?"

"Well, this is only one of a few cars that I own. I thought that you'd get a kick out of this one tonight. Only the best for my girl," Chase responded charmingly.

"Your girl?" Jules said teasingly.

"Well a guy can hope can't he?" he retorted.

They both smiled as they gazed into each other's eyes for a brief moment.

"So, are you ready for your surprise?" Chase asked like it was Christmas morning.

"You mean this isn't it?" Jules asked.

"No, this isn't it silly. I'm taking you some place special," he responded.

"Oh really? And where are you taking me?" she asked playing along.

"You'll see," Chase said teasingly.

"Come on. At least give me a hint," Jules nudged.

"Nope. You're just going to have to be patient," he responded. He was having fun teasing Jules.

"Oh alright. I'll wait if I must," Jules said mocking disappointment.

Chase reached up to the front seat, and pulled out a bottle of champagne with two crystal champagne glasses, while Tony maneuvered them through rush hour traffic.

"I couldn't stop thinking about you all day," he said as he popped the cork on the champagne bottle. Jules jumped slightly at the loud pop of the cork and they both laughed. He poured the first glass of champagne, and handed it to Jules. Then, he poured himself a glass.

"Really? I thought about you all day too," Jules replied with a shy smile.

"I got very little work done today I'll have you know young lady," he said flirtatiously.

"I'm sorry," Jules said playfully even though she wasn't sorry at all. She was happy to hear that she'd been on his mind today.

"Don't be. I haven't been this excited over someone in a long time," he said honestly.

Just then, Chase leaned in to kiss her. It was a tender kiss, which lit Jules up inside. They pulled away as the car stopped at its destination, smiling as they gazed into each other's eyes.

"Oh good. We're here," Chase announced.

Tony opened the door on Chase's side, who stepped out of the car, and held his hand out for Jules. She stepped out of the Rolls and realized immediately where they were.

"You're taking me to Madison Square Garden?" she asked surprised.

"Look up at the marquis," he suggested.

Jules looked up at the digital marquis and it read "Ringling Bros. and Barnum & Bailey Circus."

"No way, you're taking me to the circus?" she asked excitedly.

"Yep. I hope that you don't think it's too dopey. You told me at dinner last night how you loved the circus when you were a kid, and I knew that the circus was in town, so I took a chance," he said hoping that his risk had paid off.

"Are you kidding? My parents use to take me to the circus every year when I was little. I haven't been in years!" she exclaimed like a big kid. "Thank you so much for thinking of this!" she said as she hugged him tightly with her eyes lit up.

"I'm glad you're excited. I wanted you to have fun tonight," he said, happy that she was happy.

"Oh this is gonna be so much fun!" she said as they walked into the stadium holding hands.

***

Moments later, inside Madison Square Garden, Jules and Chase were in their seats watching a high wired trapeze act. It may have seemed a bit strange that they were both dressed in business suits, and didn't have any kids with them, but they didn't care. They were reliving a childhood memory.

Surrounded by children of all ages and their parents, Jules was eating cotton candy while Chase had a candied apple in his hand.

"Wow, this is bringing back so many fun memories!" Jules exclaimed.

"I'm so glad you're having a good time. I am too," Chase said.

"I wonder if we're gonna get stomach aches like we did when we were kids after eating a bunch of junk food," Jules joked.

"Hey, it'll be worth it!" Chase laughed.

"Oh yeah! A man after my own heart," Jules said.

Just then, the trapeze act ended, the lights went dark, and the whole stadium began twirling mini red flashlights that were attached to long lanyards. This was one of the big traditions that Jules had loved when she was a kid. In the darkness, the only thing anyone could see were thousands of red and white lights twirling around in the stadium.

"Ooh, I use to love this part!" Jules said as she and Chase twirled their red flashlights in the air.

Jules was having the time of her life. Chase looked over at Jules as she was laughing. He loved her laugh and her ability to not take herself too seriously. He thought she was the most amazing woman that he'd met in a long time. And he realized right then that he was falling in love with her.

***

After the circus, Jules and Chase were back inside the Rolls drinking champagne and laughing, as they reminisced about the fun night that they'd had. Jules still had her mini red flashlight hanging from a lanyard around her neck.

Tony was driving them uptown with a giant stuffed elephant sitting on the front passenger seat next to him. Chase had bought the elephant for Jules so she'd have a keepsake to remind her of their fun date.

"I still don't see how they get all of those clowns into that itty bitty car!" Jules giggled. She was a little buzzed off of the champagne.

"You really are a big kid at heart aren't you?" Chase asked rhetorically.

"Shhh. Don't tell anyone! I'm supposed to be a tough as nails attorney, remember?" Jules joked.

"Well, I'm glad that you're having fun," Chase said.

"I can't think of a better way to spend a Friday night. Besides, this was definitely the first time that I've gone to the circus VIP style!" Jules teased.

They both laughed before Chase's mood turned serious.

"Jules, I want to tell you something, but I'm a little nervous," he confessed.

"Oh come on. We just shared a huge tub of popcorn, cotton candy, candy apples, and hot dogs together. How can you be nervous around me after all of that?" Jules teased.

"Jules, I know that this might sound crazy since it's only our second date, but I think that I'm falling in love with you," Chase said seriously.

Jules stopped laughing and looked at him seriously. Had she just heard him correctly?

"I know it sounds insane since we just met, but I'm a firm believer in trusting your gut. And my gut is telling me that you're someone who's going to be very special in my life," Chase continued. Jules sat quietly as she listened to Chase's declaration.

Tony continued to drive as though he couldn't hear every word that was being said in the back seat. Over the nineteen years that he'd been a professional driver, it had always amused him how his clients repeatedly forgot that he was there. His discretion was one of the traits that made him such a good driver, and he took pride in that.

"Jules, you feel so right to me," Chase continued. "I feel like I can be myself around you, whether we're acting like serious adults or playing around like big kids. You're a breath of fresh air," he said.

"Chase, I don't know what to say," Jules said touched.

"You don't have to say anything. I just wanted you to know how I'm feeling," Chase said thoughtfully.

"These past twenty-four hours have been such a whirlwind for me since I met you. I can't remember the last time I've been swept off my feet. And we have so much fun together," she said.

"Well, there's more fun on the way," he replied still in a serious mood. He paused for a moment as if he was debating something in his head. "I'm going to have Tony drop you off at your place now, and I hope that you don't mind if I don't accompany you upstairs tonight."

"Sure, that's fine," Jules said looking puzzled. "Did I say something wrong?"

Chase looked into Jules' eyes with longing.

"No. You didn't say anything wrong. In fact, this has been the perfect evening," he said with a slight smile.

"So, why don't you want to come upstairs? It's a Friday night, and I don't have a curfew," she said trying to lighten the mood. "Maybe we can stay up all night, and I can kick your butt in Spades or Connect Four."

Chase broke out into a big grin. He loved her playfulness.

"That sounds amazing. But you and I both know that if I come upstairs, we won't be playing Spades," Chase said in an extremely sexy tone. Jules was so turned on at that moment that she forgot all about Tony's presence, and she leaned in to kiss him. He met her kiss with a familiarity as if they'd been kissing each other for years.

"Come upstairs and play Spades with me," Jules whispered seductively into his ear in between kisses. He pulled her into his arms and kissed her deeper until Jules felt like she could melt into a puddle.

"I want to come upstairs and make love to you all night long," he whispered breathlessly in between kisses.

Just then, the car pulled up in front of Jules' apartment building and stopped. They stopped kissing, and soon came back down to Earth.

"I don't want to rush things with you. I don't want to blow this. You're too special," Chase said. "Can I see you tomorrow?"

"Sorry, I'm tied up tomorrow during the day. Robin and I are bridesmaids in our friend, Mylyn's, wedding, so we're going dress shopping tomorrow morning," she explained. "But I'm free tomorrow night if you want to get together then," she offered.

"Tomorrow night it is. I'll call you in the morning to work out the details," he said.

"Sounds good," Jules agreed. She gave Chase one last kiss.

"Thank you for such a magical evening. I had a great time," she said.

"You're what made it magical," he responded. "I'll call you tomorrow."

Tony had already gotten out of the car, and he opened Jules' door.

"Okay. Goodnight," Jules said as she stepped out of the Rolls.

Chase grabbed the big stuffed elephant from the front seat and handed it to Jules. Then, he kissed her hand like a knight in shining armor before she walked off towards her building. Chase told Tony to wait until he saw that Jules had made it safely into her building. Then, they drove off into the night.

CHAPTER 6

The next morning, Jules, Maggie and the very pregnant Robin were standing together in a glamorous fitting room at the Vera Wang bridal boutique on Madison Avenue. They were wearing strapless, lavender, tulle bridesmaid's dresses, and were admiring themselves in a wall-sized mirror. Mylyn was trying on her wedding dress behind a curtain just a few feet away.

"So Magpie, how are you enjoying married life?" Jules asked.

"Married life is great! It's been a bit hectic though," Maggie said. "Elton and I had no idea how exhausted we'd be from the wedding. I couldn't believe it when we slept through most of our honeymoon. We're gonna need to visit Hawaii again since we didn't get to see as much as we would've liked."

"Oh come on. I know you two didn't just sleep the entire honeymoon," Robin teased.

"Well, no. We did manage to squeeze in some hanky panky time in between naps," Maggie joked.

"Uh huh! That's what I thought," Jules teased.

"And then, after we got back to New York, we had to move into our new place Downtown," Maggie vented. "It's all exciting stuff, but it's been one tiring thing after another."

"Well then it's a good thing that you're here having some girl time with us today," Robin said supportively.

"Totally. I feel like I've been out of the loop for the past few weeks," Maggie confessed. "So what's been going on with you gals?"

"Well, Jules went out with Robin's cousin the other night," Mylyn yelled from behind the curtain.

"Really?" Maggie squealed. "I want to hear all about that."

"Yeah Jules. How was your date with my cousin? I told you that he's a charmer didn't I?" Robin said trying to get the juicy scoop.

"Girl, that's the understatement of the year! And correction, it's dates, not date," Jules announced.

"What? You went out again last night?" Robin asked surprised.

"Let me tell you about your cousin, Mr. Chase Wilder," Jules started. "On Thursday night, we met at 'Phantom of the Opera', and then went out for dinner and dessert afterwards."

"Nice!" Maggie interrupted.

"And then, I came into work yesterday morning to an office full of roses from him," Jules said proudly.

"Oh no he didn't! Mmm, I'm liking him!" Mylyn yelled from behind the curtain.

"And as if that wasn't enough, when I got off work last night, I walked outside of my office building to find him waiting for me with a Rolls Royce and a driver," Jules swooned.

"No friggin' way!" Maggie yelled.

"Yup. And then he handed me a rose, and whisked me off to Madison Square Garden to see the circus," Jules continued.

"Wait. I'm sorry. Did you say the circus?" Mylyn yelled again from behind the curtain.

"Yep. I said the circus. And we had the most fun that I've had in years!

I'm dying to see what he comes up with next," Jules said with stars in her eyes.

"I can't believe it. Well, actually I can believe it since it's you," Robin started.

"What are you talking about?" Jules asked.

"Well, I haven't seen Chase go gaga over a woman since..." Robin said stopping herself.

"Since who?" Jules pushed.

"Since Lisa, his ex-wife," Robin revealed.

"Really? Chase hasn't gone into details on why their marriage broke up, and I didn't want to pry," Jules said.

"Well, it's a pretty sad story. Chase was head-over-heels over Lisa. He followed her around like a lovesick puppy dog. He was always surprising her with flowers and gifts," Robin continued. "He constantly came up with romantic trips and glamorous outings for them to go on. My cousin really seemed to get off on making her smile. He truly loved her."

Jules started to feel a little jealous listening to this story, and kind of wished that she hadn't asked for all the gory details.

"So what happened?" Mylyn yelled from behind the curtain.

"Well, they had been trying to start a family, but she couldn't get pregnant. They went to all kinds of fertility specialists and all of the doctors said that she was infertile," Robin explained. "They were heartbroken."

"That's terrible," Jules said feeling sad for Chase.

"Then, one day after work, Chase came home to find that Lisa had moved out of their house. She left him a letter telling him that she couldn't be married to him anymore knowing that she could never give him the child that he wanted. She said that he would make an incredible father one day, and that she couldn't stand the idea of depriving him of that," Robin said.

"That's awful. Poor Chase," Maggie said sympathetically.

"Then, she moved to Africa to work for the Peace Corp, and a few months later Chase received divorce papers in the mail. He was devastated.

Chase wasn't the same after that for a long time. That is, until you," Robin explained.

"That's such a sad story," Mylyn said from behind the curtain. "But kudos to you Jules for getting him out of his slump. Because Lord knows a good man should not be wasted!"

"Getting him out of his slump? I didn't do anything," Jules said innocently.

"Well, obviously you did something to the man. You must've put it on him girl!" Maggie joked, and everyone laughed.

"Hey, what does Charlie think about you getting wined and dined by Mr. Chase?" Robin asked.

"I don't know. I haven't seen much of Charlie these past few days. Plus, he's been acting kind of testy lately," Jules said.

"Gee, I wonder why," Maggie said, shooting Robin a knowing look, like there was an inside joke.

"I haven't figured out yet what's going on with him," Jules said.

Robin and Maggie's references to Charlie went right over Jules' head. Obviously, they suspected that Charlie had feelings for Jules even if Jules didn't realize it.

Just then, Mylyn came out from behind the curtain dressed in a stunning ivory Vera Wang wedding dress. She was smiling from ear to ear as she walked over to her friends and stood next to them in the mirror.

"Oh Mylyn. You look stunning!" Maggie admired.

"You think so? I don't look fat in this dress do I?" Mylyn asked self-consciously.

"Girl please! Of course you don't look fat. You're going to make a gorgeous bride," Jules said getting emotional and starting to tear up. She was genuinely happy for one of her oldest and dearest friends.

"Now don't you go crying 'cause then you're gonna get me started," Mylyn joked.

"My-My, with your slender shape, I can't believe that you're afraid of looking fat! Be happy that you're not walking down the aisle while you're seven months pregnant," Robin teased as she patted her pregnant belly.

"Give me time girl. Give me time! Andrew wants to get me knocked up right away, so you know it's gonna be a pretty hot honeymoon!" Mylyn sassed while snapping her fingers in the air.

The four friends starting laughing and gathered into a group hug.

***

That evening, Jules was back at home getting ready for her date with Chase. Dressed in a sexy black cocktail dress and strappy sandals, Jules was applying lip gloss to her already red lips in her bathroom mirror when her doorbell rang. She took one last admiring look at herself in the mirror, and then walked out to the living room. She smiled at seeing Chase through the peephole before opening the door. Chase took one look at her and whistled.

"Wow! What did I ever do to deserve such a sexy date? You look incredible!" he said as he leaned in and kissed Jules on the cheek.

"Thank you! I'll be ready to leave in just a second. I've gotta grab a sweater in case it gets cold," she said as she walked back into her bedroom.

"No problem. Take your time," he said. He enjoyed watching her from behind as she walked away from him. Damn, she's so beautiful, he thought to himself. This being Chase's first time inside of Jules' apartment, he began to walk around the living room to explore. He was looking at a wall full of framed pictures, when Jules walked back into the living room with a black sweater.

"Is this you?" Chase asked as he pointed to a little girl with pigtails in one of the pictures.

Jules walked over to see which picture he was referring to. "Oh yeah. That's me when I was about three years old," Jules answered.

Then, she pointed at the next picture over. "And those are my parents back in the 70s. Notice the big hair?" she laughed.

"Whoo! Your dad was old school with those bellbottoms!" Chase laughed.

"So true!" she agreed, laughing with Chase.

Then, she pointed at another picture. "And this one was taken the day that my parents took me and my cousins up to Bear Mountain. The other baby in the stroller is my cousin Miles. He lives in California now," Jules explained, touched that Chase seemed interested in getting to know more about her family.

"It looks like you have a really nice family," Chase complimented.

"Thanks. They're the best. My parents live about thirty minutes away up in Westchester County, so they're pretty close by," Jules responded.

Chase glanced around the living room. "I really like your place. It's got your style and warm personality," he observed.

"Well, thank you again. I tried to make it comfortable," she gushed.

"So, where are we headed to tonight? After 'Phantom' and the circus, I can hardly wait to see what you have up your sleeve for our third date."

"Tonight, I plan to sweep you off of your feet like never before Jules Alexander!" he proclaimed.

"Oh you do, do you?" Jules responded flirtatiously.

"Yes, I do. So fasten your seatbelt young lady. You're in for an exciting ride," he announced charmingly.

"I can't wait," Jules said excitedly.

Chase took her hand and they walked out the door.

***

That night, Chase proved to be a man of his word. He definitely impressed Jules when he brought her to his yacht, which was docked Downtown outside of the World Financial Center. She'd never been on a yacht before, so she absolutely felt swept off of her feet.

As they boarded, Jules noticed the name of the yacht that was written on the side. "Why did you name her 'Ardorous'?" she asked out of curiosity.

"Well, the word 'ardor' means enthusiasm or passion, which has brought me great success over the years. It's also the personality trait that I most respect in a person," he explained. "That's one of the reasons that I feel so drawn to you."

"Well, that explains it then," Jules said blushing. He squeezed her hand playfully as he led her onto the magnificent Ardorous.

Once on board, they watched the sun set as Ardorous cruised up the Hudson River. Chase had his chef prepare a delicious dinner of filet mignon and an incredible shrimp scampi, which they ate to candlelight on a well decorated table in the main cabin. And as if Jules weren't already impressed enough, a violinist appeared during dinner, who provided beautiful music to dine to.

After dinner, Chase led Jules out onto the deck, where there was a fantastic view of the New York City skyline that lit up the dark sky. As the yacht sailed down the Hudson, Jules started to get cold from the wind coming off of the river.

"Oh no, I left my sweater inside," Jules said, shivering.

"You don't need a sweater. I'll keep you warm," Chase said as he took off his sports jacket, and draped it around her shoulders. Then, he drew her into his arms to keep her warm. Jules was so comfortable in his embrace. She felt like she could to stay there forever.

CHAPTER 7

The next five weeks were one big romantic blur. Jules and Chase spent every free moment together as Chase whisked her off on one whirlwind date after another:

> *One Sunday afternoon, Chase picked Jules up at her apartment in a black Maserati, and drove her to brunch at the Loeb Boat House in Central Park. Then afterwards, they changed clothes and went horseback riding through Central Park. Chase was a skilled equestrian, but Jules hadn't ridden a horse since she was a kid. Chase gave her a few pointers on how to sit up and hold the reigns, but Jules couldn't stop laughing. Eventually, she got comfortable in the saddle again, and she was off and trotting along the horseback riding trail with her new beau.*
>
> *One Tuesday evening, Chase sent Tony to pick Jules up in his Chevy*

Suburban. He brought her back to his penthouse apartment on Central Park West so he could impress her with his cooking skills. He was hard at work in his spacious kitchen making dinner for Jules, while Jules sat on a bar stool at the counter drinking a glass of red wine, telling him about her day. Chase made Jules his mother's recipe for homemade spaghetti sauce. They enjoyed each other's company over dinner as they continued to get to know each other.

One Thursday evening, Jules and Chase emerged from his Rolls Royce in front of Lincoln Center. She was dressed in a stunning red evening gown and Chase had on a classic black tuxedo. They made a very attractive couple. Chase took Jules by the hand, and they walked quickly passed the large fountain on their way into the ballet.

Later that night, Jules and Chase were kissing at her front door. She was trying to say goodnight, but he couldn't stop kissing her. She used her key to open her door, and he tried to follow her inside. But Jules held firm and reminded him that he'd wanted to take things slowly. She kissed him one last time before she stepped inside and closed the door. Once inside, she leaned up against the door breathless and in love.

Early one Tuesday evening, Jules rushed down the hallway at work for another date with Chase. She walked right past Charlie's office and didn't even stop in to say "goodnight" the way that she use to. She didn't want to risk another argument with him. Charlie saw her rush by and looked at his watch, noticing that Jules was leaving work early to go meet up with Chase. He wondered how much more of this he could take.

One Monday afternoon at work, Jules had her head down on her desk, fatigued from hanging out with Chase every night. Charlie walked in to ask her something, but after he saw her head down, he didn't say anything and ducked back out of her office.

***

Then, the Wednesday evening before Mylyn's wedding, Jules and Chase were strolling arm in arm along the Promenade in Brooklyn Heights. The Promenade ran along the East River, and provided a breathtaking view of Downtown Manhattan, South Street Seaport, and the Brooklyn Bridge.

Chase stopped and looked at Jules, but he didn't say anything.

"Yes?" Jules said inquisitively.

"Jules, I'm going to go out of business," he declared.

"What? How?" Jules asked alarmed.

"I'm sorry, what I meant to say is that I'm going to go out of business if I keep dating you," he said in a half serious tone.

"Why do you say that?" Jules asked, smiling. She couldn't tell if he was kidding.

"You've got to know the effect that you have on me. I can't work. I can't sleep. I can't do anything except think about you and the next time that I'm going to see you," he said seriously.

"So what are you saying? Are you breaking up with me?" Jules asked half kidding, but half nervous that he was about to say that they needed to cool things off.

"Am I breaking up with you?" he asked with a slight laugh. "No, it's the complete opposite."

Jules relieved, started to breathe again.

"What I'm trying to say is that maybe you should marry me," Chase said looking into Jules' eyes.

"Huh?" Jules said dumbfounded.

"The way that I see it, if we're married, then I'll get to hold you every night and wake up to you every morning," he said still gazing intensely into Jules' eyes. "Maybe then, I'll be able to get some work done, so I won't lose all of my clients," he joked.

"Okay, now I know that you're kidding," Jules said, afraid to take him seriously in case it was all one big joke.

"Okay, I'm kidding about losing my business. But I'm not kidding about us getting married," Chase said seriously as he seemed to look deep into Jules' soul.

Then, to Jules' amazement, Chase took a navy velvet ring box out of his pocket and opened it. Inside was a stunning five carat cushion cut diamond ring. Chase got down on one knee and held the ring box up to Jules, where she got a full view of the brilliant diamond.

Jules gasped. She was completely caught off guard.

"I told you on our second date that I was falling in love with you. Now it's a done deal. I've completely fallen head over heels for you Jules Alexander," he said from down on bended knee to a stunned Jules.

"I know that it sounds insane for me to propose to someone that I just met six weeks ago, but you've made me feel things that I never thought I'd feel again," he continued, his voice cracking with emotion. "All I want to do is spend a lifetime making you happy and keeping that beautiful smile on your face."

Jules had started to cry as the realization of what he was saying began to sink in.

"So Miss Jules Alexander, will you do me the honor of becoming my wife? Will you marry me?" he asked.

Jules looked bewildered. Her head was spinning as tears continued to stream down her face.

"This is so crazy... but yes! Yes, I'll marry you!!!" she said excitedly through tears.

Chase stood up excited, took the ring out of the box and slipped it onto her ring finger. Then he kissed her passionately, picked her up and began spinning her around with the lights from the city behind them across the river. They laughed and laughed as he continued to spin her around and around.

***

Later that night, Jules didn't make Chase leave when he brought her back home. She unlocked her door, and led him inside holding his hand.

They started kissing in her living room in a way that they hadn't before. Their kisses were no longer tentative. Neither one of them needed to hold back or restrain themselves. Chase kissed Jules deeper than ever before. They had waited weeks to become intimate, and Jules' heart was beating so fast that she thought it might jump out of her chest.

Chase took off his suit jacket and laid it onto the couch as Jules kicked off her heels. Then, she led Chase into her bedroom. Once there, their kisses grew hungrier and more intense.

Jules was wearing a navy dress, which Chase unzipped from the back as he continued to kiss her. The dress dropped to the floor and left Jules standing in a black lacy bra and matching panties. Chase stopped kissing her long enough to admire her beautifully toned body before he covered her mouth with his once again.

Breathless, Jules pulled off Chase's tie and dropped it onto the floor. Then, in between kisses, she unbuttoned his white shirt and dropped it onto the floor as well. Jules smiled when she saw Chase's muscular chest and six-pack abs for the first time.

Chase pulled her back into another hungry kiss, and the electricity grew as their bare bodies touched. Chase had his hand buried deep in Jules' long silky hair as he drew her closer and closer to him. He instinctively wanted to get as close to her as he could get.

Then, he picked her up and carried her over to the bed as if she were light as a feather. Jules was aroused even more at how strong he was.

Chase lowered Jules onto the bed gently, and slowly lowered himself on top of her, careful not to put his full weight on her.

While he continued to kiss her, he unhooked her bra and slowly removed her panties. His hands caressed her soft skin, and he was amazed at how beautiful she was.

Feeling his skin against hers, made Jules' desire grow even more. Chase's masculinity was overwhelming. She'd never met a man like him before. They made love for hours and hours before they finally fell asleep in each other arms.

***

The next morning, Jules got off of the elevator at work, and walked down the hallway towards her office. She had a glow and a smile that could light up a room.

She stopped by Phyllis' desk before going into her office.

"Good morning Phyllis. Any messages?" she asked out of habit.

"Yes, you just got one," Phyllis said as she scribbled the message down on her message pad. Then, she ripped the message off of the message pad and looked up at Jules when she handed her the message. "Hey, you look really chipper this morning," she observed.

"Do I?" Jules said with a big smile.

"I would even say that you're glowing," Phyllis said teasingly as she held out the message.

"Really?" Jules said trying not to smile from ear to ear. She reached out with her left hand to get the message from Phyllis, when Phyllis spotted the huge sparkler on Jules' finger. She grabbed Jules' hand to get a closer look at the ring.

"Oh - My - God!!! Is that an engagement ring?" she asked just a little too loudly for the office, but she couldn't contain herself.

"Chase proposed last night... and I said Yes!" Jules said excited to spill the beans.

Phyllis jumped up and grabbed Jules into a big hug.

"Oh honey, I knew he was a keeper! Congratulations! I'm so excited for you," Phyllis exclaimed.

"Aww thanks Phyllis. That means a lot," Jules said as she pulled out of the bear hug that Phyllis still had her in. Then, she walked excitedly into her office.

***

A few doors down, Charlie was sitting at his desk in his office. He had just overheard Phyllis and Jules' conversation that Jules was engaged. Phyllis hadn't exactly been quiet when she yelled out the news, so the whole floor had probably heard her. He grabbed his suit jacket, stood up and walked out of his office. He didn't feel like working today and was going back home.

***

Later that evening, Jules was sitting in her living room typing on her laptop. She was in gray sweats and a white t-shirt, her long hair was pulled up into a ponytail, and she was wearing her red reading glasses. She had a deposition coming up that she wanted to prepare for, and since Chase had texted that he got tied up at work, tonight was a great night for her to get some work done.

Just then, her doorbell rang. Jules walked to the front door, a bit surprised since she wasn't expecting anyone. She looked through the peephole and was excited to see Charlie standing in her hallway. When she opened the door, she noticed that Charlie looked upset.

"Hi," was all that he managed to say.

"Hey! This is a pleasant surprise. Come in!" Jules said, happy to see her friend.

Charlie walked into Jules' apartment looking a bit nervous, like he had something important on his mind.

"I'm sorry for just stopping by without texting or calling you first," he said, a bit preoccupied with whatever was on his mind.

"You can stop by at time. You know that," she said trying to put him at ease.

"Yeah well, these days, I don't know if that's true anymore," he said in a serious tone.

"Can I get you something to drink?" Jules asked motioning towards the kitchen. "Right now I think I have water or water in the fridge. Sorry, I haven't had time to grocery shop this week," she joked.

"No, nothing for me thanks," Charlie said, his anger simmering.

"So what's up? What brings you by? I stopped by your office this morning, but your assistant said that you'd left. Are you feeling okay?" she asked.

"Well, not really," he said. "I heard that Robin's cousin asked you to marry him, and that you said 'Yes'," he recapped.

"Yes, you heard right. That's what I stopped by your office to tell you. Can you believe it? I'm still in shock!" Jules said still so caught up in her good news that she wasn't acknowledging Charlie's negative tone.

"So, did you stop by to congratulate me?" she asked curiously.

"No. I stopped by to tell you that we can't be friends anymore," he said.

"What do you mean we can't be friends anymore?" Jules asked taken aback. Surely he must be kidding.

"Jules, I love you," he finally said.

"I love you too Charlie," Jules replied still not understanding what he was saying.

"No. I mean that I'm in love with you," he said. "I have been since our first week at the firm five years ago."

"What?" she said surprised. Jules was completely caught off guard. She walked over to the couch, and sat down to finally hear what her friend was trying to tell her.

"At first, I didn't pursue you because you were involved with that Lance character. So, I settled for just being your friend. Then, when you dumped him, I thought that I'd get another shot. But you swore off dating altogether," he explained to a shocked Jules.

"So, then I figured that I'd wait for you to heal, and when you were feeling ready to start dating again, then I'd tell you how I felt," he said honestly.

"Oh Charlie, I never knew," she said thoughtfully. "But I thought you were happy just being friends."

"'Friends'. The kiss of death!" he said.

"Why do guys always say that?" she asked.

"Because it's true. If a woman puts a man in the 'friends' category, he can hang it up. She'll never think of him as anything more than a pal. A buddy. It's a trap that he'll never get out of," Charlie explained.

"That's not true," Jules said.

"Yes it is! In fact, a lot of times, women don't even realize that they're doing it," Charlie said exasperated. "Look, don't get me wrong. I've loved being your friend. In fact, you've become my best friend. I've had some of the best times of my life with you."

"Me too," she agreed.

"But then, you got this crazy idea that you wanted to find a husband in two months. After I got passed the insanity of it all, I thought that you would look my way. But you never even gave me a second thought. I was just good ol' Charlie, your trusty pal that you could always count on," he said, his voice starting to get louder.

"Oh Charlie!" she said.

"Not once did you ever consider me Jules! Not once! It was probably my fault for letting you put me in that stupid 'friends' trap!" he said.

Jules continued to listen to Charlie as she sat on the couch. She couldn't believe what she was hearing.

"And then, having to watch you run around town with Chico Suave for the past few weeks... Even then, I still thought that you'd wake up and come to your senses. But you never did!" he yelled.

"And now your engaged to this guy?" he said still raising his voice. "I don't understand how you could expect to marry a man that you just met a few weeks ago. You don't even know him!"

"I know him!" she yelled back as she stood up from the couch, getting defensive.

"No Jules, you don't! You can't get to know someone in six weeks. It's impossible!" he said loudly. "You and I know each other. We know cach other inside and out. And that's because we've spent practically every day over the past five years together. Can you say the same about your new fiancé?"

"Jules, you and I can finish each other's sentences," Charlie continued. "We laugh at the same jokes. We take care of each other when we're sick. We lean on each other when life gets hard. We've really been there for each other," he said. "And still you chose to marry HIM?"

Jules sat back down on the couch willing herself to calm down and to not fight with Charlie. She could see how hurt he was and she didn't want to make things worse.

"Besides, you're only marrying him to win some bet that you made with yourself that you'd get married before Mylyn does," Charlie said, sounding a bit spiteful. "Well, Mylyn's wedding is in two days. So what are you and Mr. Wonderful planning to do? Fly off to Vegas and elope tomorrow?"

"Actually, you and I haven't been communicating well lately, or you'd know that I haven't even thought about that bet since I fell for Chase," Jules explained, trying not to lose her temper. "He deserves more than that, and so does our relationship. In fact, I told him that I want a long engagement so that he and I can spend more time getting to know each other before we start planning our wedding."

Charlie just stood in Jules' living room listening. He was so worked up, and he was a little disappointed with himself for allowing himself to lose his temper.

"Charlie, I'm so sorry. I didn't know that you felt this way," she said.

"Why didn't you know? How could you not know? Maybe I should've worn a sign that said 'Charlie The Idiot Is In Love With Jules Alexander'! Would that've gotten your attention?" he asked loudly.

"Well maybe you should've just told me instead of waiting for me to figure it out," Jules yelled back. She was getting angry now.

"You know what? You're right. This is all on me for being too chicken to step up and tell you how I felt," Charlie agreed. "And now it's too late."

"I don't know what to say," she said almost in a whisper.

"I guess there's nothing left to say," Charlie said calming down. "It really is my fault. I shouldn't have waited so long to tell you how I felt. I guess you snooze, you lose, right?"

There was an awkward silence for a moment.

"But Charlie, you can't throw our friendship away. I'd miss you too much. And I need you," she said.

"You don't need me anymore. You're marrying some other guy. He can be your best friend now," he said.

Jules stood up and walked over to Charlie. He looked like he was in a lot of pain. She touched his cheek and looked into his eyes. Charlie started to lose himself in her eyes for a second, and then he caught himself and pulled away.

"Look, I feel like hell because I just lost my dream girl. But one thing hasn't changed... I want you to be happy. I still think that it's nuts that you're marrying this guy after a few weeks, but if he makes you happy, I won't stand in your way. I'm letting you go Jules," he declared.

"Charlie..." Jules started to say but Charlie cut her off.

"Look, I've gotta go. You be happy, and take care of yourself," he said.

He leaned over, kissed her on the cheek, and left. Jules didn't move. She stood stunned at Charlie's confession. She started to tear up now that it was setting in that she'd just lost one of her best friends. She missed him already.

CHAPTER 8

Friday morning, Mylyn's wedding rehearsal was in full swing in the garden of her parents' house in Scarsdale, NY. Mylyn and her fiancé, Andrew, were standing under a white wicker arch facing Reverend Shelton. Jules, Maggie, and Robin, who was now eight months pregnant, and looked ready to give birth at any minute, were standing with three other bridesmaids to the left of Mylyn. Andrew was standing opposite Mylyn with his six groomsmen. The bride and groom's parents were seated in the front row among empty rows of white chairs on a bright green lawn.

Stephen, Mylyn's eccentric wedding planner, was yelling out directions to the wedding party.

"Okay, then there's the reading... Blah, blah, blah!... Then, the soloist will sing her song... Blah, blah, blah!... And then Reverend Shelton, you'll advise the happy couple to exchange their vows," Stephen instructed.

"And now, Mylyn and Andrew have prepared their own vows that they'd like to share," Reverend Shelton rehearsed.

"Okay, then Mylyn and Andrew say their vows... Blah, blah, blah!" Stephen continued.

"Actually Stephen, we'd like to practice saying our vows now, if that's okay," Mylyn interrupted.

"Oh, okay dear. You're the boss," Stephen said a bit obnoxiously.

Mylyn turned to Andrew and looked into his eyes. Jules watched them intently, but she looked a bit sad. She was still thinking about her confrontation with Charlie the night before.

Mylyn began reciting her vows:

Andrew, besides all of the different roles that you play in my life, first and foremost, you're my best friend. You're the first person that I call when something exciting happens in my day, and you're the first person to try to cheer me up when I'm feeling down. You're my confidante, my partner in crime, and my protector all rolled into one. I have always been blessed with great friends and a loving family, but having you in my life has completed my circle. I feel so lucky that the man that I respect most in this world, besides my daddy of course, is the man that I'm marrying here today. There's nothing more special than when the person you love, loves you back.

While listening to Mylyn's vows, Jules got lost in thought trying to figure out how she could've missed that Charlie was in love with her. She started to flash back to close moments that she and Charlie had shared over the past few months:

> *Charlie poking his head into Jules' office and then walking in and plopping down into one of her chairs.*

Jules and Charlie sharing a chocolate milkshake at the diner at lunchtime.

Charlie carrying Jules into her apartment the night that she got drunk at Luke's.

Charlie covering Jules with a blanket and kissing her on the forehead as she fell asleep on her couch.

Jules touching Charlie's cheek and looking into his eyes before he pulled away during their exchange last night.

"Excuse me Missy! Hello!" Stephen yelled and clapped at Jules, who was daydreaming, and had missed Stephen's instructions to her. She snapped back to present day and looked at Stephen.

"I'm sorry, yes?" Jules asked embarrassed.

"Now that the ceremony is over, and the bride and groom are hitched, they'll start walking back down the aisle for their big exit. Then, you and Groomsman #2 will walk up to here." Stephen said as he blocked out Jules and her groomsman's steps.

"Then, the two of you will walk arm-in-arm down the aisle behind the maid of honor and the best man. Got it?" Stephen asked.

"Yes. Mm hmm. Got it." Jules mumbled.

***

Moments later, the rehearsal was followed by a rehearsal lunch that Mylyn's parents hosted for the wedding party, and for out-of-town family members, inside of their Scarsdale mansion. Mylyn and Andrew were so happy, and it made Jules feel good to see Mylyn so elated.

Jules was proud of herself for giving up that ridiculous idea to beat Mylyn down the aisle. Seeing how happy Mylyn was, made Jules feel a little ashamed that she'd even entertained the idea of competing with Mylyn's special day. Temporary insanity was all that she could claim.

In fact, she hadn't even told her girlfriends yet that she and Chase were engaged, since she didn't want to steal Mylyn's spotlight. This was her time, and she deserved to be the center of attention. So, Jules kept her massive engagement ring in her purse during the entire rehearsal.

During the rehearsal lunch, Jules took a moment to check her cell phone. She noticed that there was a text from Chase.

> *Hi beautiful,*
> *I hope that you're having a wonderful time at Mylyn's rehearsal. Sorry that I couldn't call you last night but something important came up. I'm not sure if you'll be tied up with wedding activities all day, but if you have time, can you stop by my place? I really need to talk to you.*
>
> *Love you,*
> *Chase*

Jules re-read Chase's text and started to worry that something was wrong. So, after the rehearsal lunch wrapped up, she told Mylyn that she had to run off to take care of something, but that she would see her that night at the bachelorette party.

Then, she called an Uber, and went back down to the city to Chase's apartment. She texted him from the car to let him know that she was on her way, and he texted her back that he'd leave instructions with the doorman to let her up when she arrived.

When she got to his front door, she knocked tentatively. She had a bad feeling about whatever Chase had to discuss with her.

Chase opened the door, and immediately Jules noticed that he looked a bit haggard, like he'd been up all night. He was dressed in jeans and a t-shirt, and it struck Jules that this was the most casual that she'd ever seen him look.

He smiled as soon as he saw Jules, but it was obvious that something was wrong.

"Hi. You look gorgeous," he said as he held the door open for Jules to walk in. She was still wearing the sundress and strappy sandals that she'd worn to the wedding rehearsal.

Then, he gave her a quick "hello" kiss on the lips and walked into his living room. Something was definitely wrong, Jules thought.

"Hi yourself," Jules replied, trying to sound cheerful. She walked behind him to the living room, and even though he kept standing, she sat down on one of his couches. "I came as soon as I got your text. Is everything okay?"

"Not really," he responded still standing. He looked as though he was trying to find the right words to tell Jules something important.

"Tell me what's going on," she said, trying to sound supportive. Jules had a sick feeling in her stomach, like she wasn't going to like what she was about to hear.

"Okay. Remember last night when I texted you that something had come up at work?" he asked.

"Yes," Jules responded, listening intensely.

"Well, I got a call from my ex-wife, Lisa, telling me that she was in New York. She said that she needed to discuss something with me, and she asked if I could meet her," he explained.

"Okay," Jules replied in a tone that encouraged him to go on. With Jules' history of getting cheated on, that sick feeling in the pit of her stomach started to creep up. She prayed in that brief second that history wasn't repeating itself.

"So, I met her in a lounge, downstairs at her hotel," he continued.

"And then what happened?" Jules asked.

"She told me that she's four months pregnant," he said quickly as if he was ripping off a Band-Aid.

Jules had stopped breathing. She felt the walls of her heart crashing in, and she knew what Chase was about to say next.

"And I'm the father," he said.

Jules didn't move. She just sat on the couch staring at him like she was in a bad dream.

Chase sat down next to her to continue filling her in on all that had occurred the previous evening.

"Obviously, I was shocked since the whole reason that Lisa had left me was because she couldn't get pregnant," he went on. "I was devastated when she ran off to Africa and divorced me. I loved her and I would've stayed with her no matter what. But she loved me too much to deprive me of getting to be a father one day."

As Jules continued to listen, Chase stood up and started to pace as he continued his story.

"I mourned the loss of our marriage for a long time. And it didn't help that I'd never gotten closure since she'd left so abruptly," he explained. "And then four months ago, Lisa's mother got sick, and Lisa flew back to Chicago to visit her mother in the hospital. While she was in town, she called me, and said that she'd had a chance to think while she was in Africa.

She said that she'd been wrong to just leave without saying goodbye, and she asked if I could meet her for a drink."

Chase walked over to the window and stared out of it while he relived his past.

"It was so good to see her after she'd disappeared almost two years before. She said that she'd missed me, and she apologized for causing me so much pain," he continued. "Then, we decided to have dinner in the hotel restaurant. We had a great time telling stories from the past and reliving old times. And before we knew it, emotions were running high, we ended up in her hotel room, and one thing led to another."

Jules continued to listen, not sure about how she should feel.

"The next morning, we woke up and wished each other well, and said our official 'good-bye.' Thankfully, Lisa's mother recovered, and Lisa went back to Africa to continue her work with the Peace Corp. I decided a month later to move to New York for a fresh start, and then I met you," he said and smiled lovingly at Jules.

He walked back over to the couch, and sat down again next to Jules. He looked sad and confused, and Jules' heart ached for him.

"Lisa and I had tried for three years to get pregnant. We visited all of the best doctors, and they all said that Lisa couldn't get pregnant," he marveled. "And now that I've finally moved on, and I'm about to start my life with you, Lisa shows up pregnant? It's like a bad joke."

Jules put her hand on top of Chase's and looked at him supportively.

"Jules, I honestly don't know what to do," he said in a raw and stripped down voice.

"Yes you do," Jules finally said. "Chase, you're a good man. One of the best that I've ever met. And I know that you could never live with yourself if you didn't go back to be a full-time father to your child."

Chase's eyes starting to tear up. He knew that he was losing Jules with every word. But she was right. He just hated that it was going to cost him this incredible woman.

"A child is one of the biggest blessings that a person can receive, and that child deserves to have two loving parents raising him or her every day," Jules said, her voice filling with emotion.

"There's only one solution in this situation. You have to go back to Lisa and try to give your child a loving home," Jules said with tears streaming down her cheeks.

"But, what about us? What about the life that we were planning?" Chase asked. "Does that all just go up in smoke now?"

"I think that it has to," Jules answered honestly. "I don't think that I could feel good about our relationship if it meant keeping a father away from his child."

Chase looked into Jules' eyes and knew that she was right. Her selflessness made him love her even more. It was killing him that he was going to have to let her go.

Jules reached into her purse and pulled out her engagement ring. She opened Chase's hand and put the ring in it.

"Thank you for loving me," she said tearfully. "Even if it was just for a short time."

"I'm so sorry Jules. I never meant to hurt you. That's the last thing that I wanted. I was looking forward to spending the rest of my life loving you," he replied. He took her face into his hands and pulled her in for one last kiss.

"Be happy," she said as she pulled away and looked into Chase's eyes. "You're going to be a daddy," she smiled. "As sad as we are right now, you have a child on the way, and that's incredible news. So enjoy it. Celebrate it. And go be the best daddy you can be. Make our sacrifice worth it," she said as she stood up to leave.

"Thank you Jules. Promise me that you'll be happy too. Don't stop until you find someone that'll keep a smile on your beautiful face," he said.

"Okay, I promise," Jules responded. She looked at Chase's handsome face one last time, and walked out the door. As she walked slowly down the hallway, wiping tears from her face, she knew that letting Chase go was the right thing to do. But her heart hurt so badly. She was going to miss Mr. Chase Wilder.

***

That night, after Jules had gone home to change clothes, her Uber dropped her off at a place called The Love Shack. This was the "For Ladies Only" strip club, where Mylyn's bachelorette party was being held.

After losing Chase just a few of hours before, Jules really wasn't in the mood to watch a bunch of naked male strippers prancing around in their G-strings. But, she didn't want to let Mylyn down, and frankly, she was hoping that hanging out with her girls would help to lift her spirits.

Jules walked inside the club, which was dark except for the lights coming from an empty stage. There was a dance floor in front of the stage with a disco ball hanging over it, with tables surrounding the dance floor that were filled with loads of women.

A DJ was playing Janet Jackson's *The Pleasure Principle*, which had all of the ladies bopping their heads and dancing with their friends as they eagerly waited for the show to start.

As Jules looked around the club for her friends, she was surprised to see that there were quite a few women there that were old enough to be her grandmother. "What on Earth? I better not see my Nana up in here," she mumbled to herself.

Just then, Jules spotted Maggie and Robin waving her over. They had reserved a large rectangular table that sat right in front of the dance floor. Twelve of Mylyn's other friends were already there, laughing and dancing at the table, waiting for the guest of honor to arrive.

On the table were lots of colorful gift bags from Mylyn's friends that were filled with wildly erotic lingerie. Mylyn would probably never wear most of this stuff, but she and Andrew would definitely get a few laughs out of it. There were also two big cupcake towers filled with rows and rows of multi-flavored cupcakes.

Jules walked over to the table, hugged Robin and Mylyn, and introduced herself to the other ladies that were sitting at the table.

"You guys got a great table!" she complimented Robin and Mylyn.

"The best table in the house!" Maggie yelled over the music.

"Sorry I'm a bit late. It's been a long day," Jules apologized.

"No worries. You're here now and that's what counts," Robin responded.

"Hey, do you guys know when Mylyn will get here?" Jules asked.

"She's on her way," Maggie answered. "I just texted her sister Becky, and she and Mylyn's cousins have her blindfolded so she won't see where they're taking her. They should be here in a few minutes. Becky also said to tell you ladies 'thank you' for getting here early to set up."

"Awesome! Becky has been such a great maid of honor," Maggie yelled over the music.

"She totally has!" Jules agreed, as she bopped her head to the music.

Just then, a waiter stopped by and dropped off three drinks.

"We ordered you a Midori Sour. Hope that's okay," Maggie said to Jules.

"That's perfect. Thanks! I'll probably need a few more of these before the night is over," Jules laughed, as she took a long sip of her drink.

Robin, who was the only eight months pregnant woman in the strip club was sipping on a club soda.

"Hey Jules, I got a cryptic text from Chase about an hour ago that you'd had a rough day and that I should check in on you," Robin said. "Do you wanna talk about it?"

"Well, I wasn't going to bring it up until after Mylyn's wedding, but Chase and I broke up this afternoon," Jules revealed.

"Oh no!" Maggie responded.

"I'm so sorry. I thought that you and my cousin were hitting it off," Robin added.

"We were. We even got engaged two nights ago," Jules confessed.

"What?" Maggie squealed.

"How come this is the first time that I'm hearing about this?" Robin asked, shocked.

"Because we didn't want to steal Mylyn's spotlight. So we were going to wait until after Mylyn's wedding to tell everyone our great news," Jules explained.

"So what happened?" Maggie asked. "Why did you break up?"

"Turns out his ex-wife Lisa is pregnant with his baby, and he just found out about it last night," Jules announced.

"Nooooo!" Maggie exclaimed.

"Wait, what? I'm confused," Robin said. "I thought that she couldn't get pregnant. And they got divorced two years ago, so how is that his baby?"

"Well, it turns out that by some miracle, she can get pregnant," Jules said, trying not to sound catty. "And it's his baby because they had one night together four months ago to get some sense of closure."

"Oh Jules, I'm so sorry," Robin said, pulling Jules into a hug. "You must feel like crap."

"Yep. That pretty much covers it. I spent a couple of hours at home crying my eyes out, and then I decided to put on my happy face to come here to celebrate Mylyn," Jules explained. "The past twenty-four hours has just had so much drama!"

"Wait, did something else happen?" Maggie asked.

"Well, you're not going to believe this, but how about Charlie showed up at my door last night, angry as hell," Jules stated. "He said that he's been in love with me since the day that we met, and he couldn't believe that I'd never given him a shot at being more than just a friend. He was hot because I'd agreed to marry Chase. Can you believe that?"

Maggie and Robin shot each other a look, which Jules picked up on.

"What?" Jules asked.

"Well Jules, it was pretty obvious how Charlie feels about you," Maggie stated.

"It was?" Jules asked flabbergasted.

"Oh it totally was!" Robin added. "Anyone that ever saw the two of you together could see how Charlie looked at you, and how close the two of you are."

"Really?" Jules asked again.

"Frankly Jules, we were always surprised that you never saw it," Robin declared.

"So why didn't you two say anything?" Jules asked.

"Well, at first you were with Lance, so there was no reason to say anything," Maggie recapped. "And then, you'd decided not to date for a while."

"Honestly, I thought that when you were ready to start dating again, you and Charlie would've hooked up," Robin confessed. "But, then you started dating my cousin, so again, it just didn't seem like the right time to tell you."

Jules sat still for a moment trying to process what her friends had just told her.

"How did I lose two great guys in twenty-four hours?" Jules asked.

"Well, you may've lost Chase, but you didn't lose Charlie," Maggie offered, trying to comfort her friend.

"Actually, I did," Jules said. "He told me last night that he couldn't be my friend anymore because it was too hard to just remain friends when he wants more."

"Oh please. That's just his bruised ego talking," Robin said, trying to perk Jules up. "You can get him back, especially now that you and Chase aren't getting married."

"Maybe," Jules halfway agreed. "But I don't think that it would be fair to Charlie to try to get him back unless I'm willing to offer him more than just my friendship. He drew his line in the sand by revealing his feelings for me, and if I don't feel the same way, then I'm just going to hurt him all over again."

"So then the question is, how do you feel about Charlie?" Maggie asked.

Jules thought for a second.

"I love Charlie. He's one of my best friends," Jules answered.

"Yes, but are you in love with Charlie?" Robin asked.

"Well, I don't know. I never had to think about it before. He was just always there for me whenever I needed to talk or laugh or cry. He's been my rock at work over the past year since

Lance and I broke up." Jules thought about it some more.

"I think that you were right when you said that you need to figure out how you feel about Charlie before you approach him," Robin advised. "You don't want to jerk him around."

"No, of course not," Jules agreed.

Just then, Robin's phone buzzed, causing her to look down and read it.

"Okay, look alive ladies! Becky just texted me that they just pulled up, and they're walking Mylyn in now," Robin announced excitedly.

A few seconds later, a blindfolded Mylyn was led into The Love Shack by her sister, Becky, and her two cousins. They had put a wedding veil on her head and a white, satin sash across her chest that read "Bride-To-Be" in pink letters.

Jules, Robin and Maggie waved them over. As a giggling Mylyn walked up to the table, her sister Becky said "Okay Miss Bride, get ready for your bachelorette party!"

As she took the blindfold off, all of her guests yelled, "SURPRISE!!!"

Mylyn's smile went from ear to ear as she walked around hugging all of her friends, thanking them for coming. This was her moment, and she was loving every minute of it.

Minutes later, the male host for the evening walked out onto the stage with a microphone.

"Welcome ladies to The Love Shack! It's time to get this show started, so I hope you're ready to see some incredible dancing tonight. If you ladies are ready, everybody say 'HELL YEAH!'" the announcer yelled and held the microphone out to the audience to respond.

"HELL YEAH!" the crowded club roared back.

"I can't hear you! I said, if you ladies are ready, everybody say 'HELL YEAH'" he yelled, riling the audience up.

"HELL YEAH!!!!" the club of ladies yelled back even louder.

"Ok great! So get your money out ladies, and let's get ready to have some fun!" the host yelled out.

As Jules looked around the club, there were at least fifty ladies holding dollar bills in their hands, waiting to stuff money down a G-string. She could tell that some of these women had really been looking forward to this.

"First up, we've got a fan favorite!" the host announced. "Those of you that are regulars to The Love Shack already know him, and those of you who are newcomers, will fall in love with him. Ladies I give you Slick Rick!!!!!" he yelled and walked off to his seat off the side of the stage as the ladies cheered and went wild.

Just then, the lights went down, and the DJ started to play the Rick James hit *Give It to Me Baby*. The curtain opened, and the stripper, Slick Rick, appeared on the stage wearing a cowboy hat, a black leather vest, extremely tight black leather pants and cowboy boots. He had to be around six foot four, all muscle, and his whole body was slick and shiny, as though he'd poured a whole bottle of baby oil on himself backstage.

Jules was amused at how excited all the ladies got in the club when Slick Rick appeared. It was like he was a celebrity, or something.

Slick Rick had a whole dance routine choreographed that included lots of gyrating, handstands, and all types of lewd acrobatics.

"He's so limber!" Mylyn yelled over to the music to her friends. Everyone was laughing and dancing in their seats to Slick Rick's routine.

Almost from the beginning of his act, Slick Rick started removing clothing. First, he removed his cowboy hat, twirled it around flirtatiously on his index finger, and threw it into the audience to some lucky lady, who screamed when she caught it. Then, he slowly and seductively removed his vest, and threw it to another woman, who looked like she might hyperventilate. Then, the big reveal. He ripped off his leather pants, which Jules figured must've been secured by Velcro, and he threw the pants to one of the grandmothers in the audience.

Mylyn, Jules, and the rest of the bachelorette party were laughing so hard that Mylyn's sister, Becky, fell out of her chair. They were all having a blast!

By the time Slick Rick finished stripping off his entire costume, all he had left were his cowboy boots and a gold G-string that covered an extremely long man part, which Jules mused couldn't possibly be real.

Then, he jumped off the stage onto the dance floor and started gyrating and twerking, while crazed women ran up to him and started putting dollar bills into his G-string. They ran their greedy hands over his heavily oiled muscular body, while he danced and spun around them.

As Slick Rick made his money on the dance floor, the host got back onto the microphone to announce the next dancer.

"Next up, we've got another dancer that the ladies can't get enough of here at The Love Shack! He prides himself on being a lover, not a fighter," the host announced suggestively.

Everyone, put your hands together for The Latin Lover!!!!"

The crowd of ladies went wild when The Latin Lover appeared on the stage wearing a bullfighter's costume. He had on a black matador's hat, a green and gold cape, and very tight black pants. Like Slick Rick, he was a really tall man of about six foot three, and all muscle.

Once again, the ladies watched as the exotic dancer performed his routine, and then jumped down onto the dance floor in his G-string to get swarmed by a bunch of dollar-toting adoring fans. By now Slick Rick had danced into the audience and was making his way around the club, gyrating on women who held dollars in the air at their tables.

Eventually, there had been about ten strippers to grace the stage, and they were now all making the rounds in the club, letting sexually deprived women jump onto their backs and simulate all kinds of sex acts.

Mylyn was busy feeding a cupcake to The Latin Lover and smearing white icing onto his chest, when Jules had decided that she'd had enough. This really wasn't her scene, and she'd had such an emotional twenty-four hours. All she wanted to do was go home and climb into bed.

"I'm gonna go. This has been fun but I'm really tired," Jules yelled to Robin over the music.

"Well, wait for me. I'm gonna head out too," Robin responded. "I think that this baby has had enough partying for one night," she said patting her large belly.

"Perfect! We can walk out together," Jules stated.

They said their goodbye's to Mylyn, Maggie and the other ladies at the bachelorette party, and headed for the door. It had been a long day.

***

The next morning was Mylyn's wedding at her parents' house in Scarsdale. The garden was decorated so beautifully with white roses and pink peonies. Stephen, the wedding coordinator, had really outdone himself.

The bridesmaids were beautiful, dressed in their strapless, lavender tulle gowns and Mylyn looked incredible in her ivory Vera Wang wedding dress. From looking at them, one would never guess that these ladies had been out partying it up at a strip club until the wee hours of the morning.

Seeing the love that Mylyn and Andrew shared, and what great friends they were, made Jules think more and more about Charlie. She had tossed and turned all night because she couldn't stop thinking about everything that Charlie and her girlfriends had said. And the more she thought about it, the more she realized that she had been so wrong. She shouldn't have shoved Charlie into the "friends zone" and she should've been open to trying out a relationship with him a long time ago. It was a mistake that she planned to fix as soon as possible, because she didn't want Charlie to spend another day thinking that she didn't care about him.

Jules grew more and more anxious as Mylyn's wedding day progressed. Now that Jules knew that she had to talk to Charlie, it was all that she could think about.

After the ceremony, everyone joined the happy couple for an intimate reception that took place inside of a large white tent that had been set up on the grounds of Mylyn's parents' estate. Jules had never seen Mylyn look so happy in all the years that she'd known her, and she was thrilled for her friend.

After the reception, and Mylyn and Andrew's exit in a vintage white Bentley, Jules still had Charlie on her mind. She walked over to Robin and Maggie who were sitting at one of the tables under the tent.

"Well ladies, we got our gal married off," Jules proclaimed.

"Yes, we did. And she looked dazzling," Maggie added.

"And I don't think that smile ever left her face the whole time," Robin laughed.

"So listen, I thought about what you guys said last night about Charlie, and I know that I messed up. So I'm going go find him now and fix things with him," Jules announced.

"Well, finally!" Robin exclaimed.

"You go get your man, doll. Today should be a day for happy endings," Robin advised.

The three friends then gave each other a group hug.

"I love you ladies," Jules said, still hugging Robin and Maggie.

"We love you too," Robin and Maggie both said in unison.

With that, Jules dashed off to go find Charlie.

***

About an hour later, Jules got off of the elevator at her office, still wearing her lavender bridesmaid's dress. She knew that Charlie often worked on Saturdays, as did a number of attorneys in her firm, and she was hoping to find him there. She practically ran down the hallway to Charlie's office, but all that she found was an empty office with the lights off. Phyllis, who had popped in to work for a few hours, spotted Jules and walked over to her.

"Hey, what are you doing here? I thought that you had Mylyn's wedding today. Your bridesmaid's dress is gorgeous, by the way," Phyllis stated.

"Thanks! The wedding is over, and Mylyn is now a happily married lady," Jules informed Phyllis. "I just stopped in for a few minutes because I need to talk to Charlie. Do you know if he came into the office today?" she asked a bit anxiously.

"Well, you're not going to believe this, but Charlie called in yesterday and announced that he's taking a leave of absence," Phyllis said in a loud whisper as she leaned into Jules, as if relaying the hottest gossip of the week.

"What??? Did he say why?" Jules asked worried.

"No. He just said that he needed to get away and that he's leaving town today," Phyllis relayed.

"Leaving town? To go where?" Jules asked.

"He didn't say hun. I'm surprised that you don't already know since you two are so close," Phyllis responded.

"I've been tied up with Mylyn's wedding for the past couple of days, so this is all news to me," Jules explained feeling like this was all her fault. "Well, if he calls in again, can you please transfer him to my cell? It's really important that I speak to him."

"Okay. Sure," Phyllis answered.

Then, Jules walked quickly back down the hall to the elevators.

***

Once outside of her office building, Jules ran out into the street, still in her bridesmaid's dress, and whistled for a taxi. A yellow taxi stopped and she climbed in.

"SoHo please. I'll tell you the address in a minute," Jules said to the taxi driver.

The taxi took off down the street.

Jules took out her cell phone and speed dialed Charlie.

Charlie, it's Jules. I can't believe that you turned your cell phone off. You never turn your cell

> *phone off! Listen, I'm on my way to your house right now and I really need to talk to you. I just stopped in at the office looking for you and Phyllis told me that you took a leave of absence? Look, I hate to say this on your voicemail, but I'm afraid that I won't get another chance to say this since I heard that you're leaving town today.*

She paused and took a breath. The cab driver looked at her in his rear view mirror as he listened to Jules' message.

> *Charlie, I love you too. I don't know why I didn't see it before, and you were right to walk out on me Thursday night. I've been a complete idiot these past couple of months! But please, I need to see you. Please call me when you get this message. Or if you're at your place, please stay put since I'm on my way there right now. Okay? Okay, bye.*

Jules hung up the phone as the taxi continued to race down the street.

***

Minutes later, Jules was in front of Charlie's brownstone in SoHo. She got out of the taxi and ran up the front steps, with her lavender bridesmaid's dress flowing behind her. She rang the doorbell, but there was no answer. After a minute, she rang the doorbell again, but still no answer. Then, she began banging on the door, but still no one came.

Feeling defeated, Jules sat down on the top step and put her head in her hands. How had she messed things up so badly with one of her best friends?

"Jules, you're such an idiot!" she said to herself.

Just then, an old woman opened the front door of the brownstone next door.

"Excuse me. Are you looking for Charlie?" she asked concerned.

Jules raised her head with tears in her eyes.

"Yes, but it looks like I missed him," Jules answered hopelessly.

"Well, he just left about fifteen minutes ago. Maybe you can catch him. Are you his lady friend that he's always talking about? Jules?" the old woman asked.

"Um, yes. I'm Jules" Jules said a bit surprised that the old woman knew her name, and perked up a bit. "Do you happen to know where he went?"

"He had a suitcase with him when I saw him, so I asked him if he was going away on vacation. He said that he was catching a train to Connecticut to visit his mother," the old woman offered.

"Thank you ma'am. Thank you so very much!" Jules said as she popped up from the steps with a new energy.

"Good luck to you!" the old woman yelled out to Jules as Jules ran down the steps and ran up the street towards the subway station in her flowing lavender gown.

"Thank you!" Jules yelled back.

***

Moments later, Jules got off of a subway and ran up the steps. She ran through Grand Central Station as she dodged the crowds of people, who were all walking in different directions. She stopped in the middle of the main concourse to look up at the train schedules on the huge digital black boards that hung above the ticket windows.

After spotting the train to Greenwich on the board, Jules looked at her watch to check the time, and then ran down the stairs to the Lower Level. Once on the Lower Level, she ran to Track 112 since this was the track that the Metro North train to Greenwich was leaving from.

Out of breath, Jules was heartbroken when she saw the train pulling out of the station. She was too late.

Then, Jules felt someone tap her on her shoulder from behind. She turned around and was surprised to see Charlie standing there. Without a thought, she grabbed him and hugged him hard.

"Thank God! I thought I'd lost you," she said relieved.

"I just missed my train," he said, confused. "Jules, what are you doing here? And why are you in what I'm guessing is your bridesmaid's dress?"

"I'm looking for you! And I didn't want to risk missing you by taking time to change out of this dress," she explained breathlessly with a big smile. She was so happy to see him.

"Why? I thought that you were doing wedding stuff today, and then flying off into the sunset with Mr. Wonderful," Charlie said a little too sarcastically.

"Didn't you get the message that I left on your cell?" Jules asked.

"No, my phone died. I haven't had a chance to charge it up yet," he explained. "What did your message say?"

"Charlie, I've been such an idiot!" she started, relieved to have another chance with him. "Yesterday morning, I was at the wedding rehearsal listening to Mylyn's vows, and all I could think about was you."

Jules took Charlie's hand in hers as she continued to explain.

"I don't know why I never saw it. You're my best friend. You're the one that I turn to in good times and bad," she said. "Maybe subconsciously I was afraid to take a chance with you because I was afraid of losing you if things didn't work out. It was just safer to keep you in the 'friends zone'. But the last couple of days have opened my eyes to the fact that I love you Charlie Rowland. And I'm so sorry that I took you for granted."

Charlie being cautious, wanted to believe Jules, but he didn't want to get hurt again.

"And what about Mr. Wine and Dine? What does he think about all of this?" Charlie asked, still keeping his guard up.

"That's over. We're not getting married," Jules announced. "He's got a past that he needs to deal with, and I have an incredible man in my life that I've been overlooking."

"Really?" Charlie asked perking up as if a huge weight had been lifted from his shoulders.

"Yes, really," she said. "Charlie, I've been running all over town looking for you."

"You have?" he said feeling a bit flattered.

"And when Phyllis told me that you'd taken a leave of absence and was leaving town, it felt like the world had stopped," Jules continued. "God, I've been so selfish and insensitive to your feelings, and I'm so sorry."

Charlie squeezed her hand, smiling, as she went on.

"I think that I must've had a psychotic break or something when Mylyn called to tell me that she was getting married," Jules halfway joked. "I don't know why I reacted the way that I did. I'm so happy for her, and she and Andrew make such a great couple."

"Jules, you really ran all over town looking for me?" Charlie asked, wanting to hear her say it again. He loved that she had finally realized how important he was to her.

"Yes, I totally did," she laughed. "First, I went to the office. Then, I took a taxi to your house."

"You went to my house?" he asked surprised.

"Yup. And after I banged on your door for a few minutes, your neighbor told me that you'd just left and was going to your mom's house in Connecticut with a suitcase," Jules explained.

"Ah, you met Mrs. Rodriguez. She's such a sweet lady," Charlie added.

"Yes, she is," Jules agreed. "And then, I ran down your street and caught the subway to Grand Central Station before you found me here."

"You did all of that running around in that dress? Wow, I'm really flattered," Charlie said, smiling wide. "But Jules, you didn't have to go running all over town looking for me. It's not like I was leaving town forever. I was just going to Connecticut for the weekend to hang out with my family," he laughed.

Feeling a bit foolish, Jules laughed along with Charlie.

"Hey, remember a few months ago when we were at my house watching 'When Harry Met Sally?' she asked like a light bulb had just gone off in her head.

"Yeah," Charlie responded not knowing where she was going with this.

"And remember at the end of the movie, when Billy Crystal realizes that he loves Meg Ryan, and he's running through the streets of Manhattan to get to her, and he says something like 'when you finally realize who you want to spend the rest of your life with, you want the rest of your life to start right away'?" she recited.

"Yeah, I remember that line," Charlie responded, starting to catch on to where Jules was going with this.

"Well, that's exactly how I felt today," Jules revealed.

"Really?" Charlie asked. "So, what are you saying?"

"I'm saying that I want to be with you... as more than friends," she said. "But, I don't want to rush things like I've been doing for the past two months. I want us to spend time together enjoying each other's company, and let things go wherever they lead naturally."

"That sounds like a great idea. I'd like that," Charlie agreed. "But what about your mission to get married?"

"You know, I've learned a lot over the past couple of months," Jules explained. "I don't want to make the mistake of rushing into a marriage because I'm afraid of being single past a certain age, or because all of my closest girlfriends are married. That isn't why two people should make that type of commitment."

Charlie listened intently, still holding Jules' hand, and impressed at her self-analysis.

"So, Charlie Rowland, will you agree to date me?" Jules asked cutely.

"Yes. I will," Charlie answered charmingly.

Then, he drew her in and kissed her tentatively at first. They both smiled as their kiss deepened. They were both exactly where they wanted to be.

www.ingramcontent.com/pod-product-compliance
Lightning Source LLC
Chambersburg PA
CBHW031524220925
32966CB00009B/269